RICHARD
AND
THE
VRATCH

Other Avon Camelot Books by
Beatrice Gormley

BEST FRIEND INSURANCE
FIFTH GRADE MAGIC
THE GHASTLY GLASSES
MAIL-ORDER WINGS

BEATRICE GORMLEY says, "When I was growing up in the hills around the San Fernando Valley, in southern California, some of my happiest times were spent hiking through the sagebrush with a jackknife in my pocket. Although I never actually saw a vratch, I made up stories to myself about the adventures I might have. I now hike through the woods and fields of New York with my faithful dog, Molly."

Beatrice Gormley is the author of several popular books for young readers, including *Fifth Grade Magic, Best Friend Insurance, Mail-Order Wings,* and *The Ghastly Glasses,* all published by Avon Books. She lives in Ossining, New York, with her husband and two daughters.

EMILY ARNOLD McCULLY has illustrated all five of Beatrice Gormley's Avon Camelot books. She lives in New York City.

RICHARD AND THE VRATCH

Beatrice Gormley

Illustrated by Emily Arnold McCully

AN AVON CAMELOT BOOK

RICHARD AND THE VRATCH is an original publication of Avon Books. This work has never before appeared in book form.

AVON BOOKS
A division of
The Hearst Corporation
105 Madison Avenue
New York, New York 10016

Library of Congress Cataloging in Publication Data:

Gormley, Beatrice.
  Richard and the vratch.

  (An Avon Camelot book)
  Summary: Richard's artistic ability helps him foil the scheme of an unscrupulous scientist, who seeks to capture the small dinosaurs hiding in the hills behind Richard's house.
  [1. Dinosaurs—Fiction. 2. Artists—Fiction] I. Title.
PZ7.G6696Ri   1987   [Fic]   87-1121

First Camelot Printing: October 1987

To Lois and David,
who grew up with me in vratch country

Contents

1

The Call of the Wild

Dropping his many-bladed Swiss army knife into his jeans pocket, Richard hurried toward the back door. He thought he turned the doorknob quietly, but his mother called to him from the laundry room.

"Richard? If you're going hiking, I'd like you to get someone to go with you. All right?"

Richard hesitated. He'd gotten into trouble yesterday when he came back from a long hike and his mother realized he had been exploring the hills above their house by himself. "Okay," he called back. "Okay" didn't necessarily mean "Okay, I'll do what you said." "Okay" could just as well mean "Okay, I understand— you want me to get someone to go hiking with me. But be reasonable, Mom. Who could I get?"

As if she had heard his thought, Mrs. Hayes called, "Tony Heckman might like to go for a climb."

Before he could hear any more helpful suggestions that were supposed to be taken as instructions, Richard stepped outside and closed the door. He glanced across the street to see if Tony Heckman was around, but the

Heckmans' cement driveway was blank. He looked up to the end of the street, from which Tony often swooped down on his bike at what seemed like seventy miles an hour. The street was empty. Good. In case his mother asked, Richard had looked for Tony Heckman.

Lifting his head, Richard gazed at the hills rearing into the sky. The Lagarto Grande hills, people called them, but Richard thought of them as mountains. When he had first caught sight of them, just before they moved here from Pleasant Acres, his scalp tingled. A phrase from a song came to him: "purple mountains' majesty."

Click.

The sound of a pebble hitting the end of his driveway made Richard turn. Across the street a boy Richard's age, with dark shaggy hair and low-slung jeans, picked another pebble from his handful. He tossed it a little farther up Richard's driveway. *Click—rattle*.

So far, Richard had avoided Tony because he reminded Richard of a boy in Pleasant Acres who had tried to pick fights with him. Mom didn't seem to realize what kind of boy Tony was, though. She just wanted them to be friends because she was friendly with Mrs. Heckman, because Tony's little sister went to the nursery school where Mom taught.

Click—rattle. Richard could see that Tony was trying to get his attention, but he pretended not to notice. Instead of walking up the short street to the end, as he had planned, and hiking up the dry creek bed in the canyon, Richard turned. Crossing his backyard, he walked along the ivy-covered chain-link fence to the side of the hill. It seemed more interesting to climb the fence, anyway, as if he were escaping. Digging the toes of his

2

sneakers into the holes where the ivy was thinnest, he vaulted the fence without even scratching his wrist.

As he scrambled up the bank of the crumbly, rusty-colored rock, Richard grasped a sage bush to pull himself up. The pungent sage smell came off on his hands, and he breathed it deeply into his lungs. Ahh. The adventure started here.

Back in Pleasant Acres, adventures did not happen. Pleasant Acres was nothing but rows and rows of new houses on tiny lots, each with its bright green doormat of a lawn and its skinny new tree tied to a stake. Richard rode his bike down flat street after flat street, looking for adventure, but the best thing he had found was a new park with more scrawny, braced trees. Nothing hidden, nothing wild.

Part of Richard's ideas about adventure came from his favorite book, *The Call of the Wild*. With his Swiss Army knife in his pocket, Richard felt like the outdoorsman of the Klondike, John Thornton. "With a handful of salt and a rifle he could plunge into the wilderness and fare wherever he pleased." Inside his head, as if it were a tape deck, Richard played parts of the book.

His legs pumping steadily up the steep path, Richard brushed through dry, scrubby bushes. No one used this path, he was sure—no human beings, anyway. Last week, on this very spot, he had raised his head, panting from the climb, to see a deer.

The deer stood perfectly still for a moment, staring at Richard. *Is he dangerous?* the animal seemed to be asking itself. The deer's dusty brown blended into the sun-scorched grass and brush—if it had stopped a little farther away, Richard might not have seen it at all. Only

3

its soft eyes moved. Then it bounded off the trail with a crackling of twigs, and it was gone.

A deer, a wild deer, living right here in the hills above his house! Not in a zoo, not even in a national park like Yosemite. No one had planned for the deer to be there so Richard could see it—it was just part of life here in Lagarto Grande. Who knew what might happen this afternoon?

At the top of the first rise Richard glanced back. From this height he could see that the houses on his street, Vista Drive, were set on terraced lots, rising like steps along both sides of the road. A purple car crawled up the street and into the driveway of the house below Richard's. That must be Mrs. VanNest, coming home from the newspaper, the Lagarto Grande *Grande View*, where she worked. The white snout of her overweight dog, Snowball, poked out of the car's back window.

Last week someone had stuck a cardboard sign, PRIZE PIG, on Snowball's doghouse. Pinned to the sign was a red ribbon: Second Prize, Pomona County Fair. Richard had heard Mrs. VanNest complaining to his mother about it. "Of course I know it wasn't Richard—it was that Heckman boy. Second prize!"

Richard turned back to the trail. "Plunge into the wilderness," he muttered. He knew, of course, that these sparsely covered hills, here at the edge of the desert in Southern California, didn't look anything like the country in Alaska where John Thornton roamed with his fierce dog, Buck.

The Boy Scout camp Richard had gone to last summer, in fir woods and meadows, had actually looked like John Thornton country. At summer camp, though,

4

Richard could never go off by himself. That was the important thing—once he was up in these hills, he could do exactly what he wanted.

His eagle-sharp eyes missed nothing, thought Richard as he noted the large, reddish bush tucked into a fold of the hill. Out of sight under the bush—a low tree, really—he could rest. He could also eat the provisions in his back pockets: peanut butter and crackers and an apple. He would cut up the apple with one of the blades on his Swiss Army knife.

Panting and a little dizzy from the steep climb, Richard turned again to look down. Now he could see the whole valley: the spread of housing developments with their blue dots of swimming pools, the cluster of stores and gas stations along the main street of Lagarto Grande, and the green rectangles of the high school football field and the park. On the other side of town the freeway was hidden under a dirty fuzz of smog, like a long dust curl.

The Hayeses' house and the VanNests' house were hidden by the shoulder of the hill, but he could see the Heckmans' and a figure slouching on their driveway. Oh, no. That was Tony Heckman. If Richard could see him, Tony could see Richard, and he might follow him.

Richard scowled. Even though Tony's family had lived on Vista Drive before the Hayeses, Richard felt that the hills were *his,* not Tony's. Well, let Tony try to follow him—he wouldn't catch a seasoned dweller in the wild like Richard.

John Thornton, outdoorsman and explorer, watched expressionless as the foolish greenhorn plunged into the desert wastes with only a day's supply of water. Later

Thornton would come across Heckman's bleached bones and shrug. Such was the law of the wild.

Richard climbed on up the bare, rocky spine of the hill. He would find shelter farther on, someplace that Tony Heckman didn't know about. His legs bent and straightened, bent and straightened, lifting him up—up—up. At the top of this rise the path met the fire-break, a dusty road scraped up one side of the ridge and down the other.

Richard turned onto another spur of the ridge, away from the firebreak. Examining the trail behind him, he was glad to see that the crumbly rock held no footprints. Even if Tony hiked this far, he would think Richard had gone up the firebreak.

The trail sloped down now, and Richard's street and the town of Lagarto Grande were out of sight. There were only the hills covered with sagebrush, with dead stalks of yuccas sticking out like coatracks, and the canyons dark with wooly-looking oaks.

Who knew, thought Richard as he pushed through the brush, what he might find in these hills? A forgotten Indian tribe. An ancient temple, full of treasure.

In a saddle between hilltops Richard found another large bush, just off the trail. He crawled under its branches, brushing through the blade-shaped, reddish leaves. Dead leaves crackled under his hands and knees. But there was a patch of ground under the bush, he saw, that was *not* covered with leaves.

On his hands and knees, Richard tensed like a dog sniffing another dog's traces. Someone had been here before him and brushed the leaves away. Look, there was a picture scratched in the smooth dirt. A sort of cartoon of part of an animal with small forelegs—a rabbit? It was hard to tell.

Anyway, someone had been here before Richard. Whoever it was, Richard hated him. What was he doing in Richard's hills? Richard started to back out of the bush to go farther on, but stopped. What good would that do? He might actually run into the person, which would be worse than finding a picture. Rubbing out the doodle with his fist, Richard brushed leaves over the dirt. Then he settled himself with his legs crossed.

Richard had to get up on his knees again to pull his provisions out of his back pockets, the crackers a little crushed. Then he unfolded the large blade of his Swiss Army knife and cut the apple in quarters. Carefully he carved out each piece of core, wiped the blade on his jeans, and ate the quarter.

But he couldn't feel comfortable, knowing that someone else had sat under this bush and doodled a picture. Finishing his snack quickly, Richard crawled out from under the bush. A few yards away the ground fell away into a canyon, hidden by oaks. What was that noise coming from down there?

Richard stood still on the trail and listened. The wind rustled the sagebrush, but that wasn't what he had heard.

There it was again: a bird or animal call. A low, grating sound like a rusty iron hinge. *Vratch.*

And again: *vratch, vraaatch.* There must be a whole family of vratches—whatever they were—in the canyon. Richard guessed it was a large bird like a crow, but he knew animals didn't always make the noise you ex-

7

pected from them. Squirrels, for instance, sometimes screeched instead of chattering. Frogs might yelp instead of croak. Geèse could make a barking sound, almost like dogs.

Richard wished he could climb down into the canyon and explore. But the afternoon light was fading. John Thornton knew better than to get caught in this savage country after sundown. He'd better hit the trail.

Back up at the firebreak, Richard saw that the sun was dropping toward the hills across the valley, shining orange into his eyes. It was later than he had thought.

Richard expected to make better time on the way back, since it was downhill. But actually he found himself going more slowly because the downhill trail seemed steeper. His feet slid on the crumbly rock, and his knees grew tired from braking his weight at every step.

Squinting against the low sun, and concentrating on not falling downhill, Richard didn't notice the boy waiting for him on the last slope.

"Hey, your mom's looking for you."

Startled, Richard raised his head, slipped, and flapped his arms to keep from falling. "What are you doing here?"

"It wasn't my idea," said Tony. "Your mom called my mom to see where you were, and my mom made me go look for you." Turning, he slid down a straight stretch of trail as if he were on a skateboard. Then he stopped and waited for Richard, eyeing him curiously. "What are *you* doing up here?"

Richard thought Tony meant he didn't want Richard hiking in *his* hills. Could the picture under the bush

8

have been Tony's? he wondered. He asked in a cautious tone, "Do you hike up here a lot?"

"Why would I do that?" Tony looked surprised. "There's nothing to do in the hills."

Richard scrambled downward, past the other boy. "You never know what you might find," he said over his shoulder. "Like a picture of a strange animal that someone drew under a bush."

Tony hurried after him. "You're nuts. What kind of animal?"

"Well," said Richard. Why had he mentioned that? Now he felt he had to come up with something interesting. "Whatever animal the person saw. For instance, they might see an animal that everyone thought was extinct." Excitement built up in his chest, pushing the words out. "Animals like dinosaurs."

"That's dumb," said Tony as they clambered down the cut into Richard's yard. "Dinosaurs, sure. Oh, yeah. That sounds like this dumb science fiction movie I saw last night."

"I didn't say they *were* dinosaurs. I just said they might look like dinosaurs."

Tony seemed ready to argue some more, but the conversation was over. Mrs. Hayes was waiting outside the back door with her arms folded. *"Richard.* Do you know what time it is? Look, it's practically dark!" She motioned him in the door with an angry sweep of her hand. "Tony, thanks for going after Richard."

"No problem," Tony called back, trotting down the driveway.

"Yes problem," muttered Richard, embarrassed. It

9

wasn't as if Tony were any older than he was or even any better behaved.

"No lip, please," said Mrs. Hayes. "I don't know why you didn't ask Tony to go with you in the first place, like I told you to. Now you are *not* going up there again."

2

A Boy Needs a Dog

In the kitchen Richard leaned against the refrigerator, looking away from his mother. Not wanting to think about how mad she was, he thought instead about the yellow reminder slips stuck on the refrigerator door, tickling the back of his neck.

Mrs. Hayes paced from the table to the sink and back again, the line between her eyebrows deepening. "I hope you understand that I'm angry because I was worried. Don't you have the slightest idea why Dad and I don't want you to go hiking by yourself? Just imagine, if a brushfire had started while you were in the hills alone—there was a terrible fire in the Malibu Hills last week. Or what if you had met some kind of maniac up there? What if you had broken your ankle?"

Maybe all of that could have happened at once, thought Richard as he watched the twitching hem of his mother's denim skirt. He could have met a maniac, and fallen and broken his ankle trying to run away from him, and then the maniac could have set a brushfire and

11

run off chuckling evilly, leaving Richard helpless to escape the crackling flames and billowing smoke.

"Anyway, you are *not* going up in those hills again, that's for sure."

That was the second time, Richard suddenly realized, that his mother had said that. He stared at her, pushing himself away from the refrigerator. "I can't go in the hills again?" He couldn't believe his mother really meant that. If he couldn't go up in the hills, they might as well have stayed in Pleasant Acres.

The shock must have shown in Richard's face, because his mother looked more sympathetic. "I just don't think it's safe, by yourself. But we'll discuss it when your father gets home."

Richard hung around the driveway, bouncing an old tennis ball and watching the sky over the valley turn darker and darker blue, until his father's car pulled in. He was hoping to get to Dad first and explain his point of view. But his father shut his eyes and waved his hand in front of his face as if he were shooing away fruit flies. "Give me five minutes, Rich. I've had a more or less tough day."

After Mr. Hayes had laid a folder of papers on the kitchen counter and loosened his tie and kissed Mrs. Hayes, she told him in a serious tone what Richard had done. His father walked into the family room as he listened, followed by Richard and his mother, and sank into an armchair. Laying his palm on his forehead as if he were testing for fever (always a bad sign), he gave Richard the same lecture that his mother had just given him.

"But nothing *did* happen," protested Richard. "I'm

sorry Mom got worried, but I was all right—I was just fine. You guys don't want me to have any fun."

"You don't seem to get the point, Richard," said his mother. "The point isn't that we don't want you to have fun. The point is for you to have *safe* fun. What if you *had* broken your ankle? How would we know where to look for you? You'd be helpless."

"No, I wouldn't. I could scootch home on my rear end."

Richard's father smiled faintly, massaging his forehead under his thin gray hair. "That's absurd. Your mother's right—you can't go hiking by yourself. Get someone to go with you, like the kid across the street—the Heckman kid."

"That's what I *told* Rich." Folding her arms, Richard's mother sat on the arm of the sofa.

"That's not fair—it's just like saying I can't go hiking at all." Richard stood squarely in front of his father's armchair. "Tony doesn't even like to hike. It's not fair!"

"*You* are not in any position to talk about what's fair," said his mother. "I told you not to go hiking by yourself, and you disobeyed me without even talking it over."

Richard's heart sank. He wouldn't even get a chance to explore that canyon. Canyon Vratch, he would have named it.

"Just a minute. I think I have a solution." Mr. Hayes stopped rubbing his forehead and snapped his fingers. "If Richard got a dog, he'd have a ready-made companion to go on hikes with him."

"Yeah!" The minute Dad said it, Richard saw him-

13

self again as John Thornton in *The Call of the Wild*, striding into the wilderness with his mighty dog, Buck, beside him. "Yeah, a dog could protect me, and if I broke my ankle or something he'd come back and—"

"A dog," said Mrs. Hayes with surprise. She pursed her lips at Richard. "I'm not sure he'd be willing to take care of it. Dogs are all right, but *I* don't want to be the one to feed it and take it out and so on."

"I think Rich is old enough to be responsible for a dog," said his father. "Of course, it would have been a nuisance to have the dog cooped up in that tiny yard in Pleasant Acres, but here it would have the run of the hills."

And so would I, thought Richard. "Yeah, he'd get all the exercise he needed, all right."

Richard's mother still looked doubtful. "I see what you mean about a dog, but I wonder if Rich really needs to have his own dog. Maybe he could . . . he could borrow Snowball from the VanNests."

"Snowball!" exclaimed Richard and his father together. Mr. Hayes added, "That fatso dog would have a heart attack at the top of the first hill."

His mother laughed. "Okay, you're probably right. Anyway, now that I think of it, I'm sure Gloria VanNest wouldn't let her precious puppy go off on adventures with Rich."

"So I get a dog," said Richard, to pin his parents down. "You mean, tomorrow?"

His mother hesitated, then nodded. His father said, "It'll be good for you to have the responsibility. And besides—a boy should have a dog."

*　　*　　*

When Richard climbed on the bus for his class's field trip the next morning, he couldn't think about anything except getting his dog. He was surprised, now, that he hadn't thought of it before, as he imagined himself having all those John Thornton adventures. After all, that's what *The Call of the Wild* was about: a dog. A huge, strong dog, Buck was, with a mighty heart. Devoted to his master. Once Buck had won a bet for his master by hauling a sled-load of half a ton, and once he saved his master's life by pulling him from the icy rapids of a river.

Richard's thoughts were interrupted by a boy dropping into the seat beside him. A boy with jeans slung low on his hips, chewing a wad of gum as if it were tobacco. "Hi," said Tony.

"Hi," said Richard coolly, not sure he wanted a long bus ride with Tony Heckman. Tony was a rib-jabber, as Richard knew from the time Tony had sat beside him in an assembly. He wished his dog, Buck, were already here, trained to growl if anyone tried to poke him.

"I'm getting my own dog," he found himself saying, as if just mentioning a dog would make Tony keep his hands to himself.

Tony looked interested. "What kind? If I got a dog, I'd get a Doberman. Dobermans don't mess around. If somebody bothers you, they'd tear his arm right off. *Chomp*—bye-bye, arm. Yeah, I'd get a Doberman." He put his feet up on the seat in front of him. "What kind of dog are you getting?"

Richard looked casually out the window as he answered. "A mixed breed. He's part German shepherd, part St. Bernard. He looks like a wolf, only bigger."

"Oh, yeah?" Tony raised his eyebrows respectfully. "What're you going to call him? If I got a dog, I'd call him Thor."

"Buck," said Richard, relaxing in his seat. Maybe his ribs would be safe for this bus ride, anyway. "I'm calling him Buck."

At the museum Richard wasn't sorry when Tony stayed beside him. Maybe the other boy didn't know many kids, either, he thought. "Did you just move here this year?"

Tony shrugged. "Yeah. We move a lot."

"Shh! Shh!" Their teacher, Mr. Hassler, was glaring in their direction.

Clearing her throat, the museum guide smiled around the group. "Now that we've learned how scientists discover the bones of dinosaurs and other prehistoric animals, we're going to get back into our time machine and zoom forward a few million years. Not quite to the present—to five hundred years ago, when the only people around here were the Lagarto Grande Indians. Follow me into the pottery room, please."

"Let's go," hissed Tony. He jerked his head toward the opposite door.

"Go where?" Richard glanced at Mr. Hassler, but the teacher was turned away, pulling another boy down from a glass case. He hurried after Tony. "Go where?"

Tony frowned at Richard's sneakers slapping on the tiled floor of the hall. "Keep it quiet." He slunk along the wall like a cat. "You don't want to look at pottery, do you? I'm going back to the saber-tooth—"

Just then a door swung open in front of them, and

Tony pulled Richard back against the wall. ASSISTANT DIRECTOR, said the sign on the door a few inches from Richard's nose.

"What're you—" began Richard, but Tony cut him off with a poke in the ribs.

"—exciting that you're doing this fieldwork in Lagarto Grande, Dr. MacNary," said a woman's crisp voice. "The museum will be glad to assist you in any way we can—aside from the money. Your field, cryptozoology, isn't one of the areas we support. Now if you were doing archaeological work on the Lagarto Grande tribe itself—"

"But this relates directly to the Indians!" A man on the other side of the door sputtered. "My theory is that the Great Lizard Spirit was an actual animal. *Is* an actual animal! I'm holding the picture right in front of you"—there was a sound of paper rattling—"can't you see it?"

"Dr. MacNary." The woman's voice was still calm but with a hint of warning. "You are showing me a photo from a nature calendar, taken in the Lagarto Grande hills. I see a thicket of sagebrush and what *might* be an animal with large eyes hiding in the bushes. Dr. MacNary, there is no reason—certainly no *scientific* reason—to think that animal is what you call an ornithoid dinosaur. It could just as well be a fawn."

The man gave a harsh laugh. "A fawn. That's how you explain away the ornithoid. I suppose you think those are fawns in the Indian pottery designs."

"I have a great deal of work to do this morning, if you'll excuse me." The door hiding Tony and Richard jerked as the woman tried to pull it shut and the man held it open.

Then the door swung shut suddenly, revealing a man with a mottled, boiled-looking face and light frizzy hair. Dr. MacNary held a calendar page in one hand and a black briefcase in the other. "When I have found the ornithoids," he told the closed door, "and done my experimental work on them to prove that I have discovered a new species, this museum will go down in history as an obstacle in the—" He caught sight of the boys flattened against the wall, and his eyes bulged even more. "What are *you* doing?"

Richard was so startled he couldn't speak. But Tony, still flattened against the wall, tried a smile. "Oh, hi. We were—we were just looking for the rest room."

For a moment the man said nothing, looking down at Tony and Richard as if *they* were a new species of worm. Finally he spoke. "Mm-hm. You thought the rest room was behind the door."

"We didn't mean to spy on you or anything," said Richard in a breathless voice.

Tony gave him a scowl and another jab in the ribs. Dr. MacNary laughed his short, sarcastic laugh. "No? Excuse me, kiddies, but I think you did. And I think I know who sent you." His pale eyebrows lowered, and he spit out a single word. "Mounce."

"Mounce?" asked both the boys.

With a knowing nod, Dr. MacNary opened his briefcase and put the calendar page away. "Mounce, that second-rate ornithologist, who would give anything to discredit me." His purplish lips twitching, he bent toward the boys. "How much is Mounce paying you?"

Richard edged along the wall, away from the man's stale breath. He opened his mouth to explain that they didn't know Mr. Mounce, and they wouldn't spy on anyone for money if they did, and—

"Not that much." Looking unconcerned, Tony stepped away from the wall. "Mounce is a cheapskate."

Smiling as if he suspected that, Dr. MacNary took his wallet from the inside pocket of his suit jacket and pulled out a five-dollar bill. He waved it in front of Tony's eyes. "This much?"

Tony shook his head. Richard began, "To tell the truth—" but he stopped as he noticed Tony's elbow coming toward his ribs again.

"So don't tell Mounce anything," said Dr. MacNary. "Understand?"

Shocked, Richard watched Tony pocket the bill and nod. His face was blank.

"No, I take that back." Dr. MacNary's bulging eyes gleamed. "Tell Mounce that *no one* is going to stop me from getting my hands on the ornithoid." His free hand clenched and unclenched. 'No one." Turning, he strode toward the exit. But as he pushed the door, he glanced back at the boys with a hard look that showed the whites at the bottoms of his eyes.

As Dr. MacNary disappeared, Tony snickered. "What a fruitcake. Five bucks!"

"*Were* you spying for this Mounce guy?" demanded Richard.

Tony gave him a disbelieving look. "Don't be dumb. I don't know Mounce from Adam. Dr. MacNary must be one of those crazy scientists who thinks everybody's out to steal his secrets."

"Then why'd you let him think we were spies? If he's going to look for that animal in the hills, he might see me up there." Richard wished he had gone to the pottery room with the rest of the class.

"Calm down," said Tony. "By that time you'll have your dog, Buck, and if Dr. MacNary lays a finger on you, Buck goes for the jugular." He grabbed his throat to demonstrate. "Anyway, nothing's going to happen— unless we don't get back before Mr. Hassler finds out we're gone." Looking toward the exit, he added, "In a way, it's too bad we can't follow that MacNary guy. I bet he's doing something weird he doesn't want anyone to find out about."

As they loped back down the corridor, Richard decided not to tell Dad or Mom about Dr. MacNary. They would think he was just the kind of maniac they were worried about Richard meeting in the hills.

"Here." Tony nudged him through a doorway marked POTTERY ROOM.

Mr. Hassler caught sight of them and beckoned impatiently from the other side of the room, but Richard had just remembered something Dr. MacNary said. Something about the animals in the pottery designs.

The last of their class was trickling out of the room, past the teacher. Richard walked along the display cases as slowly as he dared, peering at the pottery. These bowls only had sun and rain cloud designs on them.

"Richard." Mr. Hassler stepped toward him, frowning.

Richard quickened his steps past the last case—and then came to a dead stop. This must be the design Dr. MacNary had been talking about. A line of people and animals, animals like kangaroos with ostrich heads, dancing around a pottery jar. "What's that, Mr. Hassler? What're those animals?"

The teacher gripped Richard's arm and steered him toward the door, which Tony was already whisking through. "That, as you would know if you had been here listening to the guide, is the Great Lizard Spirit, after which Lagarto Grande is named."

"Sorry," said Tony from the doorway. "We had to go to the rest room."

The teacher gave him a skeptical glance. "Do you boys think we came to the museum to go to the rest room?"

"No," said Richard, although that wasn't the kind of question that really needed an answer. He twisted his head over his shoulder to get one last look at those animals. What had Dr. MacNary called them? Ornithoids. Little front legs with claws held up like hands, powerful hind legs, long thick tails sticking straight out behind.

A lot like the animal he had found doodled in the dirt under the bush.

3

Buck

After school that afternoon, Richard's mother drove him to the county animal shelter. "Now remember, Rich, this is going to be *your* dog, not mine."

"Yeah, I know, Mom." Richard fingered the dog collar on his lap, one Snowball had outgrown. Mrs. VanNest had given it to him when she heard he was getting a dog.

"That means you feed the dog, you brush him, you take him for walks." She turned into the parking lot beside the low concrete-block building. "I don't need something else to do—I teach nursery school, I play tennis, I'm helping Mrs. VanNest with the school page of the newspaper. And I'm especially busy this week, working with the nursery school kids on the program for Parents' Day, making sure the mothers finish the costumes—"

"Okay, okay, Mom." Jumping out of the car, Richard trotted into the animal shelter. A din of yapping and yipping burst out at him, along with a smell of dogs and disinfectant. But the noise and the smell seemed exciting to Richard because they meant he was going to get a dog of his own. Buck.

There were a few other people in the shelter, strolling along the rows of cages and peering at the dogs. "There's a nice golden retriever," said Richard's mother behind him. "Over here, Richard." She motioned him to a cage where a honey-colored dog with short wavy hair and floppy ears pushed its nose against the wires. "Good dog," said Mom, holding out her hand. The dog wagged his tail, his brown eyes gazing hopefully at them.

"I don't know about this one." Richard was sure this wasn't Buck. He could imagine what Tony would say if he came home with a "good dog" like that. On the other hand, in the next cage there was a sleek, muscular Doberman with its front paws up on the wires, snarling. Tony was probably right—a dog like that could take someone's arm off. And it might not be someone *else's* arm.

Hurrying past the Doberman, Richard thought at first that the next cage was empty. He turned to the other side of the kennel, then stopped and looked again. An animal sat hunched in a back corner. What kind of dog was that? Medium-small, with a thick body and short brown coat. Its flapped ears hung limply, instead of cocking back and forth like the golden retriever's. Was it sick?

"Here, boy." Richard snapped his fingers at the creature, curious to see it closer.

As the lumpy dog stepped toward Richard on long legs, he noticed that its front paws barely seemed to touch the cement floor. Maybe it was lame—maybe it had been hurt. There was something unusual about the way its dark eyes were looking at him.

Behind him Mrs. Hayes clicked her tongue. "The poor thing. What kind of a pitiful mongrel is that? Come on, Richard, don't get its hopes up."

But Richard was stooping down to the strange dog's level, holding out his hand for it to sniff. As he stared into its eyes, his mother's voice seemed to come from far away. The animal looked at him with a steady, searching gaze. As if it was sizing him up, thought Richard with wonder. He was seized with a longing to measure up, to be the kind of boy this animal could trust.

"Richard, are you crazy?" His mother yanked his hand back from the wires, and the peculiar dog hobbled back to its corner. "You shouldn't let that strange dog touch you. It looks to me like it might be diseased—see how dry its coat is? I don't know why the shelter didn't just put it to sleep when they brought it in."

At Mrs. Hayes's yell one of the shelter workers had started over to them. "You okay, kid?" he asked Richard. "That mutt don't seem like he would hurt anyone, and he's had his shots, but you shouldn't stick your hand into the cage."

"I wonder why the shelter put this dog out for adoption," said Mrs. Hayes. "No one's going to take a homely thing like that."

The worker shrugged. "It does look a lot like a turkey in a dog suit, don't it? But we have to give them all a chance. You never can tell who's going to like what."

Richard was leaning with his arms folded against the

wire, looking at the creature crouched in the corner. It looked back at him with its large, dark eyes.

Suddenly Richard hated the way his mother and the shelter man were talking about this dog. He hadn't thought much, when he came to the shelter, about what happened to dogs who weren't adopted. But of course he knew. And this weird-looking dog didn't have a chance of being chosen, as his mother said.

"*I* like this dog," Richard heard himself say in a loud voice.

There was a silence behind him, and then Mrs. Hayes gave a short, astonished laugh. But she spoke in a sympathetic tone. "I can see you feel sorry for this poor dog, Rich. I do, too. But you can't do anything for him. How about it—do you want the golden retriever?"

"As a matter of fact," said the shelter worker, "the golden's out of the running. That guy at the desk is already filling out papers on him."

Mrs. Hayes clicked her tongue in disappointment, but Rich didn't care. He just wished the weird dog would stop staring at him like that. It wasn't Richard's fault that the dog officer had caught it. It wasn't Richard's fault what was going to happen to it.

His mother moved to the other side of the kennel. "Look, Rich. This spaniel seems very friendly. I always liked spaniels—more than most dogs, anyway."

But Richard was staring into the strange dog's eyes again, remembering the part in *The Call of the Wild* where John Thornton first meets Buck, and saves his life. The mighty Buck hadn't looked so great at that point, either. He was in terrible shape, starved and beaten almost to death. But after John Thornton took care of him, he turned out to be a terrific dog. And of course he was devoted to his master.

Richard's mother was at his shoulder again. "It's better not to brood about it, darling," she said in a low voice. "Come see what you think of the spaniel."

"I want to get this dog."

"Oh, Rich." She shook her head. "You have such a good heart, wanting to save this miserable creature. But that wouldn't really be the best thing for him." His mother spent several minutes explaining that a sickly dog wouldn't be any fun for Rich, and probably this dog would have to go to the vet a lot, which would cost money that the family needed for other things, and in the end the dog would probably die anyway, and think how sad that would be.

While his mother was talking like this, Rich kept his head down, leaning against the wires of the cage. Every now and then he glanced across the cage at the strange dog. It was always looking back at him, turning its head from one side to the other.

"Five minutes to closing time," announced the kennel worker.

"Listen, Richard." His mother bent over to look in his face. Her tone was resigned, as if she felt she should try a little longer to talk him out of it, but she knew it was no use. "I just can't see why you're so set on getting this ugly, pitiful dog. You do understand that you're the one who has to take care of it if it needs special care?"

Richard nodded, not listening very closely. What *was* it about the strange dog's eyes? His chest felt tight.

"And if the dog isn't able to go on long hikes at first, you'll have to adjust to what it can do?"

"Yeah, Mom." As the shelter worker opened the cage and slipped a lead over the dog's head, Richard knelt and buckled Snowball's outgrown collar around its neck. The thick metal-studded collar hung loosely. So did the strange dog's skin, Richard noticed.

Mrs. Hayes went to the counter to fill out the papers. "This dog must have been terribly mistreated by its former owner," she said to the man waiting on her.

He nodded. "His tail looks like it got broken and healed the wrong way. And he don't put much weight on his front legs. No idea who he used to belong to, though. The cops picked him up in the Sew-Sew Shoppe."

Richard's mother laughed in a puzzled way. "The fabric store? You mean he walked in with some customers?"

The man laughed, too. "No, it was a lot more peculiar than that. Someone broke into the Sew-Sew Shoppe in the middle of the night and set off the alarm. When the police got there, there was nobody in the store but this dog, standing in a pile of zippers. The cash register wasn't even touched. They said it looked like the dog broke in to steal zippers." He chuckled. "This mutt could use some new clothes, all right."

Richard glared at the man. This guy was talking about *his* dog. "I'm going to wait in the car, Mom. Come on, Buck."

Buck rolled his eyes up at his new master. As if it were an effort for him, he wagged his thick tail from side to side three times before he followed Richard out of the shelter.

As their car pulled around the last steep curve of Vista Drive, Richard spotted Tony swooping downhill on his bike, into the Heckmans' driveway. He hoped Tony would go into his house. But when the other boy saw the Hayeses' car, he zipped across the street, screeching to a halt beside the car door. "Did you get your dog?"

"Tony," said Mrs. Hayes, leaning toward Richard's window, "that was quite dangerous, the way you rode your bike right behind the car. What if—"

Tony, peering into the backseat, paid no attention. "What's *that*?"

"My dog, Buck." Richard cleared his throat. "He's kind of sick right now, but he'll shape up."

For once Tony was too surprised to make any smart remarks. He just stared as Richard let Buck out of the backseat. "That's a dog?" he said finally. "A cross between a German shepherd and a St. Bernard?"

Richard stared at Buck, too, wishing now that he had chosen the spaniel or even the killer Doberman. Why *had* he picked this lumpy animal? There was a reason, but he couldn't remember it.

Then something struck him about the dog's odd shape. If you took away the fur and the flap ears, and shortened the front legs, what would he look like? He would look a lot like the designs on the Indian jars—the Great Lizard Spirit.

"A cross between a teddy bear and a turkey, if you ask me," Tony went on.

Richard was glad to have a chance to jab Tony in the ribs. "Sh! My mom doesn't know."

"Know what?" asked Tony, still in a loud voice.

Beckoning, Richard led Tony around the edge of the front yard. "Come on in back," he whispered. "I'll explain everything." Buck walked stiffly beside him, poking his head forward at each step.

"Hey, piggy!" Tony called down into the VanNests' yard, where Snowball lay on her side in front of her doghouse. "Oink, oink, oink!"

The sowlike white dog raised her head and sniffed the air. Then, to Richard's surprise, she struggled to her feet. Running to the concrete wall below them, she put her paws up and whined.

"Relax, piggy," said Tony.

"She's all upset because she smells Buck." Richard was pleased because the way Snowball was acting worked into his story. "If you were a dog and you smelled a dinosaur, you'd get pretty upset, too."

"A dinosaur—sure." Tony bent down to sniff Buck's back. "Pyew. He just smells like a dog—and like that stuff they mop rest rooms with."

"Yeah, that's because he's been in the shelter. But a dog, like Snowball, can smell his real dinosaur scent underneath. Dogs can smell a lot better than we can, you know."

Sitting down on the patio on the bench around the pepper tree, Richard went on with his story. "See, these animals—I call them vratches because they make a noise like *vratch, vratch*—have been hiding in the hills ever since the white man first came to Lagarto Grande."

"Oh, sure." Tony dropped into a patio chair. "A bunch of animals that big could run around the hills for years, and no one would notice them. Sure."

"That's just what they're afraid of," said Richard in a serious tone. "They're afraid somebody's going to find them and put them in a zoo. Somebody like Dr. MacNary. So now they don't go out of their canyon unless they have a disguise on, like this dog suit."

Tony looked at Buck and then at Richard with his head on one side, grinning as if he were humoring his little sister. "You mean they make their own disguises?"

Richard hadn't thought about that, but now he realized it fit in with what the man at the shelter had told them. "Yeah. They're very smart—it's like they have a little civilization going in that canyon. They sew their disguises out of dog skins, from dogs that get killed by cars. But they have to steal the zippers. That's how Buck got caught. The cops found him in the Sew-Sew Shoppe in the middle of the night, standing on a pile of zippers."

By now Tony was hooting with scornful laughter. Richard could see the other boy thought he was a nitwit, but somehow he couldn't help going on with the story. "Of course the cops don't know all this I'm telling you. They think Buck just happened to wander in with a burglar."

Tony snorted and rolled his eyes. "Of *course*. Oh, yeah."

"And you know the pictures on the jars in the museum," added Richard as another idea struck him. "The Indians must have thought these little dinosaurs were the Great Lizard Spirit."

"Oh, sure." Tony stood up, hands on his hips. "How come the Indians saw them and white people didn't?"

"Because the Indians treated them right—they brought

31

them gifts and stuff. But the vratches know we'd catch them and put them in cages, so no white person has ever laid eyes on them.''

"You're full of it,'' said Tony. "You're as bad as that guy in the museum—Dr. MacNary.''

"Excuse me, boys,'' Richard's mother appeared at the sliding door. "Tony, your mother's calling you.''

"If you told *him* all that junk,'' continued Tony, strolling toward the driveway, "he'd probably believe the whole thing. What a fruitcake.'' As he rounded the corner of the garage, he tossed a last remark over his shoulder. "If I were you, I'd take that loser mutt back and trade him in for a real dog.''

4

Hidden Animals

Sitting in the fernlike shade of the pepper tree, Richard studied his dog. He wouldn't have admitted it to Tony, but Buck did look pretty bad. "We have to fatten you up, Buck. Wait right here—I'll get some dog chow."

Richard knew his mother had bought a bag of dog chow on the way home, but he couldn't find it anywhere in the kitchen. "Mom?" He went out to the front yard to look for her. She was standing at the edge of the terrace with her arms folded, talking to Mrs. VanNest in the driveway below. The neighbor was leaning against her car, sunglasses pushed up on her head so that she seemed to have two sets of eyes.

"It's a Lagarto Grande Community Education class, you mean," Richard's mother was saying.

Richard was about to interrupt and ask about the dog chow when he was startled by Mrs. VanNest's answer. "Yes, but this is completely different from most of those classes. Hon, this Dr. MacNary is working on the *cutting edge* of science. And we have him right here in Lagarto Grande!"

Richard stood with his head bent, scuffing the gravel path with his sneaker. Dr. MacNary, teaching a class in Lagarto Grande?

"And the name of the course is Cryptozoology?" asked Richard's mother.

"That's right. It means *the science of hidden animals*. Isn't that delightful? The whole course will be fieldwork— searching these hills for an undiscovered species. Starting a week from Tuesday."

Richard stiffened. Searching these hills! *His* hills. Not just Dr. MacNary, but a whole class.

"It just doesn't seem very likely to me," his mother was saying. "How could an animal that large go undiscovered? It'd have to be in disguise!" She laughed. "What proof does he have—did he find tracks or something?"

Mrs. VanNest laughed back in a kindly way. "Much better proof than tracks! He has an actual photograph; he told me when he brought in the course description. So this is our chance to take part in a real scientific project!"

Shaking her head, Mrs. Hayes smiled. "I'll think about it."

"If I were you," insisted the neighbor woman, "I'd call Community Ed and sign up right now. The class will be announced in the *Grande View*, but it'll be filled up fast, it's such an exciting opportunity. We're going to comb these hills with a fine-tooth comb and mark the ground as we cover it with red tags on stakes. Very methodical. 'Every rise and canyon,' Dr. MacNary says."

"I don't see how I could take the time off, but thanks so much for telling me, Gloria. Excuse me, I think Richard wants to ask me something."

But Richard had forgotten what he wanted to ask. He was staring into space, feeling sick. Comb the hills with a fine-tooth comb! Every rise and canyon! Some wild place the hills would be, when Mrs. VanNest and Dr. MacNary got through with them.

The thought of Dr. MacNary and all the people in his class crawling over the hills reminded Richard of something that happened last summer. He had gone to the kitchen to cut himself a piece of a homemade chocolate cake with white icing. Lifting up the plastic wrap over the cake, he noticed tiny holes in the icing. Then he noticed little black ants scurrying in and out of the holes and a thread of ants trailing down the side of the cake and across the counter to a crack in the wall.

Richard's skin crawled. The sight was bad enough, but there was a funny smell, too, a whiff of something under the buttery vanilla of the icing and the chocolate of the cake. Almost a chemical smell. Ants.

"Richard." His mother shook his shoulder. "Didn't you want to ask me something?"

It turned out that she had put the dog chow bag in the broom closet because it was too big to fit in a kitchen cupboard. Scooping a couple of cups of chow into the new dog dish, Richard noticed the picture on the bag. A nice normal dog—a golden retriever.

Richard carried the dish out to the patio and set it down on the flagstones in front of Buck. "Here you go. Eat up." He couldn't help thinking, though, that no matter how much weight Buck put on—even if he got as fat as Snowball—he still wouldn't be shaped like a regular dog.

Buck looked at the pan with his head on one side. He picked up a piece of dog chow in his jaws, but immediately he let it fall out again.

"What's the matter with you?" Richard was worried. "You've got to eat—your coat's all loose." A disturbing thought came to him: What if Buck was really sick, too sick to eat? It was okay to make up wild stories for Tony, but the fact was that Richard had brought home a poor, funny-looking half-starved dog, and now he had to take care of him. Richard was sure John Thornton wouldn't give up on a dog just because he looked ridiculous.

"Look, Buck—good." He pointed to the pan of hard brown lumps. "Mm, good food for dogs."

Buck turned his head away.

Richard felt desperate. "You dumb mutt, can't you even eat?" He snatched up a piece of dog chow and popped it into his mouth. "Good, see?" He chewed the coarse-grained lump. "Really, it's not bad. Sort of like stale bread."

But Buck seemed to have lost interest in the dog chow. He pushed himself to his feet and shuffled to the edge of the patio where a line of ants were scurrying from their anthill to the corner of the house. Putting his nose down to the anthill, he began to edge along the line.

At first Richard smiled. It was funny the way dogs were so interested in ordinary little things, like ants. Then he realized that as Buck's muzzle moved over the line, the ants were gone, except for a stray here and there. Buck was *eating* the ants.

Feeling his jaw go loose, Richard watched Buck clean up a line of ants several feet long. He had to poke his muzzle under the barbecue grill to reach the last few. Richard remembered John Thornton's words about *his* Buck: "Never was there such a dog." That was certainly true of Richard's Buck, too.

Then, as if he might have hurt Buck's feelings, Richard reached down and patted his shoulder. It didn't feel the way he expected. Buck in *The Call of the Wild*, Richard recalled, had muscles like steel springs. This dog's muscles felt . . . sort of spongy. Frowning, Richard tried to feel Buck's shoulder again, but the dog moved aside as if he would rather not be touched.

"Maybe you're too thirsty to eat dry food, huh?" Dogs needed plenty of water, Richard remembered. He went back to the kitchen for a bowl, filled it at the hose, and offered it to Buck.

Buck was thirsty, all right. Dipping his muzzle into the bowl, he raised his head straight up as if he were going to howl. Richard heard the water gurgle down Buck's throat. What was that glinting under his jaw? Richard bent forward to see better, but the animal quickly lowered his head. It must have been the buckle on his collar.

Never was there such a dog, thought Richard.

At dinner that night Richard remarked to his parents, "Hey, you know what Buck eats?" He described how Buck had licked up the whole long line of ants.

His mother and father looked at him with raised eyebrows. "A dog might eat a horsefly that was biting him, now and then, but he wouldn't eat ants," said his father.

"I'll show you. Here, Buck." Richard pointed to a large black ant staggering across the floor with a crumb. "Ant! Nice ant. Eat ant, Buck. Mm."

Buck shuffled over to the ant and bent his head. "Oh, my goodness! He *is* going to eat it," said Richard's mother.

Then Buck glanced up at Mrs. Hayes, leaning against the kitchen counter, and over his shoulder at the kitchen table where Mr. Hayes was sitting. He shuffled back to Richard's feet and sat down.

With a laugh, Mrs. Hayes went back to scraping garbage into the sink. "So much for our anteater disguised as a dog!"

Richard opened his mouth to protest, but the growling of the garbage disposal cut off conversation. By the time she switched the disposal off, his mother was onto a new topic. "Rich, Mrs. VanNest asked me if you might have something you'd written for school, like a poem or an essay. She was looking for something to fill up the school page of the *Grande View.*"

"We haven't done anything like that yet," said Richard.

"What about a picture, then? I told Mrs. VanNest you liked to draw, and she said a picture would be fine. Maybe one of the pictures you taped up on the wall in your room?"

"Aw, Mom, they aren't that good." What Richard really meant was that he didn't want to give them away. Especially the one of the hills. He was proud of the way that one had turned out, showing the folds in the earth spreading out from the top of the ridge. "I'll draw a new one for her, if she wants."

Richard's father, who had been leaning under the edge of the table to study Buck, spoke up. "Maybe it's just that he's not feeling well, but there's something strange about this dog. Every other dog I've known was more or less friendly."

Dad was right, thought Richard. Normally, dogs *liked* to be touched. Dogs nudged you with their noses, and jumped up on you, and put their muzzles in your lap so that you would rub behind their ears or under their chins. Dogs rolled over so that you could scratch their stomachs. As Mrs. VanNest had showed Richard with Snowball, they *really* loved to be rubbed right on the big bone in the middle of their chests. Of course with Snowball, it wasn't easy to find that bone, or any bone, under the pads of fat.

Quickly, before Buck could dodge him, Richard bent and braced one hand on the animal's back. He placed his other hand at the base of Buck's throat, feeling for the lump of his breastbone. But his fingers met something else—something small and hard and flat buried in Buck's dry fur. Then Buck's throat throbbed with a low, grating sound, and Buck twisted away from him.

"Get away, Rich!" His mother's hand flew to her mouth.

"He didn't bite me, Mom." Richard sat up, trying to act calm, although his own heart was thudding. "He just doesn't want to be touched."

Mr. Hayes shook his head. "I don't know how you pick them, Rich. This dog isn't going to be able to go hiking with you for a while, and that was the whole idea of getting a dog. And aside from that—well, he looks more or less like a dog you'd get at a discount store, on the bargain table.''

"You mean like those shorts I got you once?'' Mrs. Hayes' eyes twinkled. "The ones marked Slightly Irregular?''

Richard's father nodded ruefully. "Mm-hm. The shorts with only one leg. *Slightly* irregular.''

When Richard had heard that story before, he thought it was very funny. But now he didn't laugh. Looking down on the top of Buck's dull brown head, he wanted to protect him from his mother and father and Tony and the people at the shelter and everyone else who would make fun of a strange-looking dog. "Buck can't help the way he looks.'' He stood up to take Buck to his room, where no one could laugh at him. "Come on, boy.''

Still studying Buck, Mr. Hayes went on in a serious voice. "Do you think he's all right, Sue? Look at the way he's sitting, as if he's uncomfortable. And the fact that he doesn't seem to want to be touched. Maybe he dislocated a shoulder or something.''

"I think he'd be whimpering if he were hurt,'' said Mrs. Hayes.

Richard snapped his fingers. "Come on, Buck.''

"Still,'' said his father, 'if he doesn't seem better Monday—no, Monday's Veteran's Day. If he doesn't seem better by Tuesday, I think you should take him to the vet and get some X rays on him.''

Leading Buck to his room, Richard was surprised to find himself talking to the dog as if he could understand. "Never mind what they say, Buck. Once you get some

rest and some meat on your bones, you'll be terrific.''
He had always thought it was idiotic when he heard
Mrs. VanNest talking to Snowball: ''Want to go ride-
rides with Mummy in the car?'' All the time Mrs.
VanNest was talking, Snowball would lie on her side
with her eyes closed, only a twitching ear showing that
she might be listening.

But Buck watched with his dark eyes, blinking, as
Richard showed him around his room. He pointed out
his bookcase, with one shelf just for the pieces of
quartz and mica he had found in the hills, and the desk
that used to belong to his older cousin Ted, with Ted's
initials carved into the top.

''See, this top drawer is where I keep my Swiss Army
knife,'' said Richard. ''It has a regular knife blade, two
screwdrivers, a can opener, a punch thing. . . .'' He
opened all the blades for Buck and then folded them in
again, while Buck watched with his head on one side. It
was strange, thought Richard, that Buck didn't cock his
ears back and forth while he was listening. His ear flaps
hung limply.

''And this is your bed.'' Richard pointed to the floor
pillow beside his bed, big enough for a dog to curl up
on. ''Want to have a rest?''

That must have been just what Buck wanted, because
with a low throaty sound he lowered himself onto the
floor pillow. He crouched there for a moment with his
legs tucked under him. Then, glancing up at Richard, he
rearranged himself so that he was lying on his side,
curled up.

''Richard!'' His father was calling from the kitchen.
''Telephone!''

41

To Richard's surprise, it was Tony. Without saying hello, the other boy started in. "You probably think somebody would believe that crock about Buck. Well, nobody would, even if they were really dumb, because if your dog were really a—what do you call it?—a vratch, a little dinosaur, then he'd have those little front legs, right? Like little arms and hands."

"I guess so," said Richard.

"Yeah, sure he would. Then how can his dog suit have those long front legs, like dogs have?" Tony gave a short, triumphant laugh. "It wouldn't work if they were just stuffed with cotton or something, would it? He couldn't walk on them."

Richard wished he hadn't told Tony that story. All right, it was dumb. But why was Tony still thinking about the vratches, anyway? The trouble was, once Richard started making up something like that, it was hard to stop. "No, it's not just stuffing." He paused, letting the explanation pop into his head. "The way they do it is, they make long bones out of wood, like the bones in a dog's leg. Then they put the bones inside the legs of the suit, with padding to look like muscles, and when they put the suit on, they hold onto the top of the bones. See?"

"It'd be like walking on stilts, the front legs." Tony spoke slowly, as if he were picturing it.

"Right," said Richard eagerly, in spite of himself. "Or like people on skis, holding ski poles."

A scornful snort came out of the phone. "You should go to my sister's nursery school and tell stories to little kids. You're full of it." The line clicked roughly.

Richard's face burned. Stalking into the family room,

42

he flopped on the sofa. The roars of laughter from the TV seemed to be aimed at him, a boy stupid enough to tell Tony Heckman the spacey things he imagined. Richard wished he had a friend in Lagarto Grande, a friend who liked *The Call of the Wild*.

5

Spies

As soon as his eyes opened the next morning, Saturday, Richard rolled over and hung over the side of his bed to see how Buck was.

Buck seemed to be asleep—at least, his eyes were closed. But he was in a peculiar position. Instead of curling up on the pillow or stretching out on his side the way dogs do, Buck was hunched in a crouch. Sort of like a hen on a nest, thought Richard.

As he watched, one of Buck's large dark eyes opened. For just a second the animal, staring at Richard, seemed frightened. He let out a growl almost like a croak. Then, seeming to recognize Richard and relax, he wagged his tail slowly.

"Good boy," said Richard. "Good old Buck. Want some breakfast? Let's see what there is." He swung his legs over the side of the bed. "Come on, Buck." He made encouraging little noises for Buck to follow him.

Pulling a sweatshirt over his pajamas, Richard tiptoed out to the kitchen. He noticed one of his mother's yellow sticky notes on the refrigerator door as he opened it: *Tues. p.m.—Buck to vet.*

Richard helped himself to Chinese spareribs, left over from last night. The half carton of slimy vegetables he left on the shelf. "Do you like spareribs, Buck? Sit, boy."

Buck slowly eased himself into a sitting position, but when Richard held out a sparerib, he turned his head away. Again Richard felt a pang of worry. Tucking an extra fortune cookie into his sweatshirt pocket, he led Buck out the patio door. "Maybe we'll find some more ants."

Richard sat down by the barbecue grill to eat his spareribs, but a crunching noise in the geranium bed behind him made him turn his head. "Buck, what are you doing?"

At first Richard was afraid his pet was eating the geraniums—that would give Mom a fit. But no—Buck was nosing under the leaves, picking something out of them and swallowing it with a lift of his muzzle and a quick crunch.

Hurling his sparerib bones up the bank into the sagebrush, Richard stooped and pushed aside the geranium leaves. Three or four round brown shells, the size of cherries, rolled onto the flagstones. "Snails?"

Buck gulped down another snail, gazing at him as if to ask, What do you think of this?

"It's okay," said Richard, suddenly worried that Buck would stop eating. "Forget I said anything. Look, here's some more." He scooped up the snails he had shaken from the leaves and dropped them in front of Buck. "Go ahead, eat them."

While Buck gobbled the snails, one after the other, Richard took the fortune cookies from the pouch pocket of his sweatshirt, broke it open, and pulled out the thin strip of paper. *He who treads on the tail of the dragon, reaps misfortune.*

Richard popped the pieces of the fortune cookie into his mouth as he strolled around the garage to the driveway. What kind of misfortune? An uneasy feeling came over him.

Tilting his head back, he gazed up the canyon at his hills. Today was clear and cool, a good day for a hike, but of course Buck wasn't strong enough to keep up with him yet. A frown tightened Richard's forehead. Maybe Buck wouldn't be well even before Dr. MacNary led his class over the hills, next week. Maybe the hills would be spoiled by the next time Richard got up there. That would be misfortune, all right.

Now that Richard thought of it, he was afraid that Dr. MacNary had already been looking around in the hills. "Who else would doodle an animal that looked like the Great Lizard Spirit?" he asked Buck, who had followed him to the driveway.

Richard's eye was caught by an object hurtling down the steep street—Tony, he realized with annoyance. The other boy swooped calm-faced into the Hayeses' driveway. "What's happening?" When Richard shrugged, he went on, "We've got that five bucks. We could rent some movies or something."

After the way Tony had talked to him last night, Richard was surprised that he was acting friendly. "Yeah, maybe we could. . . . Hey, you know that guy Dr. MacNary? He's going to ruin these hills." Richard didn't expect Tony to care that much, but he found himself explaining how Dr. MacNary was going to lead a whole class over the hills, marking them with stakes and red tags, searching every rise and canyon. "The stupid thing is," he finished, "it's all for nothing. An imaginary animal."

"I'd feel sorry for any animal *he* finds," remarked Tony. "He's probably the kind of scientist that carves up animals in his laboratory." As he said this he leaned toward Buck, making a gruesome face. Buck edged behind Richard.

Richard wished Tony hadn't said that, although he was afraid it was true. "If only someone could talk Dr. MacNary out of searching the hills . . . Maybe my dad would—"

"No, you've got the wrong idea." Leaning back on his bicycle seat, Tony tossed his shaggy head. "You don't *talk* to a guy like that. You know what we should do?"

"What?" Richard was surprised at the "we."

"We should make this MacNary guy *sweat*." Tony pushed his jaw forward as he said the last word. "Instead of asking him very, very nicely please not to wreck the hills, we should jump *him* first." Lifting the front wheel of his bike by the handlebars, Tony thumped it down on the pavement.

"Don't be dumb. How could we do anything to *him?*" But Richard felt a smile twitching the corners of his mouth. "What do you mean—what could we do?"

A gleam came into Tony's eyes, and a slow smile like Richard's spread over his face. "Spy on him."

At first Richard was excited about the idea. "Yeah! If

we got evidence that he's doing horrible experiments on animals, we could call the SPCA. Maybe even the police.'' Then he realized there was a hitch. ''How are we going to spy on him when we don't even know where he lives?''

''The telephone book,'' said Tony in a tone that meant Richard wasn't too sharp. He swung off his bike, dropping it on the driveway. ''Come on.''

In the house, they took the phone book from the kitchen to Richard's room. Buck, crouched on the floor pillow, watched as they spread it open on the desk. After an argument about how to spell MacNary—McNary? MacNerry?—they looked it up under all the possible spellings they could imagine. There was no MacNary in the Lagarto Grande phone book.

''You think you're so smart!'' exclaimed Richard, remembering something. ''I bet I know why he isn't in this phone book. It's been here since the summer, and probably Dr. MacNary just moved to Lagarto Grande.''

''Shoot!'' Tony scowled. ''We could get his phone number from Information, probably, but that wouldn't help.''

Then Richard thought of another way they might find out where Dr. MacNary was staying: ask Mrs. VanNest. ''You'd better do it,'' said Tony. ''She hates my guts.''

At the VanNests', Richard knocked with the wood-pecker door-knocker, wondering what he would say if Mrs. VanNest asked why he wanted to see the crypto-zoologist.

But Mrs. VanNest didn't ask, because she thought she already knew. ''He's such a fascinating young man! Dr. MacNary is staying at the Lagarto Palms Apartments—do you know where that is, across from the park? But don't pester him, hon, if he says he doesn't have time to chat. Dr. MacNary is giving a speech Monday at the Cryptozoological Association meeting in Riverside, and I know he's working on it. It's quite an important speech—cryptozoologists from all over the Southwest will be there.''

When Richard reported to Tony, the other boy's face lit up. "All *right!* Let's go. *We* won't pester him. Oh, no.''

"You stay here, Buck," Richard told his pet. He hated to leave Buck alone, but Buck certainly couldn't run along behind his bike like a regular dog. "I'll be back pretty soon.''

Buck wagged his tail, as if he understood.

" 'Bye, turkey," said Tony. To Richard he added, "Why does he wag his tail that way? Like he just learned how to do it.''

Already halfway down the hall, Richard pretended he hadn't heard. "Mom, we're going for a bike ride," he said as he paused in the kitchen.

His parents looked up from their eggs and coffee and newspaper. "What about Buck?" asked Mr. Hayes. "Did you take him outside this morning?''

"And did you feed him his breakfast?" asked Mrs. Hayes.

"Yeah, I did." Richard thought of Buck crunching up the snails. "He'll be fine in my room.''

A few minutes later the boys were on their bikes, coasting back and forth down the zigzags of Vista Drive. Squinting against the wind, Richard felt excited to be going spying with Tony, and he was pleased because he had gotten the information from Mrs. VanNest without giving anything away. It wasn't until they were all the way down in the valley, pedaling past the baseball diamond in the park, that Richard began to wonder what he and Tony thought they were doing. He remembered his fortune cookie message. Was bothering Dr. MacNary like treading on the tail of a dragon?

Tony, ahead of Richard, stopped with one foot on the curb and stared across the street. Two scraggly palm trees leaned across each other in front of the pink two-story apartment building. "Here we are," he said loudly.

"Yeah, but now what?" asked Richard. "What if he's on the second floor? We can't just knock on his door and say, 'Excuse me, can we come in and spy on you?' "

Tony didn't answer, except to beckon Richard to follow him. Rolling across the street, they pulled their bikes up the steps to the entrance.

"Why don't we put them in the bike rack down there?" whispered Richard, pointing.

Tony shook his head. "Might have to make a quick getaway."

There was an open doorway into an area with mail-boxes and door bells. "Here, see? MacNary, 1D." Tony tapped the name on one of the mailboxes. "So he *is* on the first floor, wise guy."

"But this is locked." Richard tugged at the glass door leading into the building.

"But that doesn't matter," said Tony, "because we're going to look in his window from outside."

"So why did we have to haul our bikes up here, then?" Richard felt jittery, and he was annoyed that Tony seemed to think he was in charge.

Pushing their bikes into the bike rack after all, the boys slipped into the bushes that surrounded the apartments. They were good bushes for hiding in, nice and thick, the kind with red berries. And thorns, thought Richard as they poked through his jeans.

The boys edged farther along the side of the building, trying not to get stuck by thorns any more than they had to. "Ow!" said Tony. "Somebody should clip these bushes. Okay, here's the first window. Give me a hand up."

Richard made a stirrup with his hands, boosting Tony while he hoisted himself up so his elbows were resting on the window ledge. "Can you see him?"

"Um—I don't think this is his apartment. Unless he has a girlfriend." Tony jumped down.

"Give me a hand, now. I want to look." Hauling himself up until his chin was level with the bottom of the window, Richard cupped his hands around his eyes to shut out the light. Through the sticks of a bamboo shade he could see into a small kitchen.

Right across from the window were the sink, stove, and refrigerator. Actually, Richard couldn't see the sink because it was overflowing with dirty dishes and pans. Between the sink and the window was a small Formica table. There was an ashtray with several cigarette stubs in it, and bright pink lipstick on the cigarette butts. "No," he whispered, jumping down. "That jerk couldn't have a girlfriend."

At the next window, Richard stooped to boost Tony again. Tony stayed up there, saying nothing, until Richard's hands began to go numb.

"Well?" whispered Richard. "Is *this* his place?"

"I don't think so." Tony eased himself down. "I don't see any cages. Unless they're in back."

"Let me look." Richard stepped into Tony's interlocked hands. Again there was a bamboo shade in front of the window, and Richard had to squint through the sticks. In this room the sink and counter were nearly bare. On an open shelf above the sink there were rows of soup cans, with the labels all turned to the front. The only thing on the table was a large manila envelope.

Then the picture taped to the refrigerator caught Richard's eye. It was as big as a poster—a blowup of a smaller photograph, judging from the grainy look. Gray-green sagebrush cut through by a narrow, rocky trail. That could have been taken right up in the Lagarto Grande hills, thought Richard. My hills.

The picture puzzled Richard, because Dr. MacNary didn't seem like the type to appreciate nature. And besides, there wasn't anything dazzling about this picture—no waterfall, no sunset, no giant redwoods. Just the feathery gray-green of sagebrush bushes.

"You weigh a ton," complained Tony below him. "Hurry it up, will you?"

Richard didn't answer. He squashed his nose against the window, trying to make out a shape in the sagebrush. Was that an eye, a large, dark, gleaming eye? The picture reminded him of a kind of puzzle he used to like, ones with a caption like, *Can you find the six elephants hidden in this picture?*

Only this was the one ornithoid hidden in the picture. Richard's heart thumped. *Ornithoid*—you might expect Dr. MacNary to give a wonderful animal an ugly name. It was a vratch, a real vratch. An animal covered with

52

small silvery feathers, but not a bird. There was one of the small hands. And the eye—the dark eye gazed at Richard as if it could see right into him. Richard felt a great longing to be near this creature, to sit and watch it for hours. He felt he was on the point of understanding something very important, if only . . .

Then he had to squeeze his tired eyes shut. When he opened them, he couldn't make out the vratch in the picture anymore. "Oh, no," he groaned.

"If you don't get down," said Tony, "I'm going to drop you."

Jumping onto the dirt, Richard stared at Tony wildly. "That *is* Dr. MacNary's place! That must be the picture Dr. MacNary had in the museum, only bigger. Remember—the one he was talking to that lady about? And he's not crazy. That *is* a—an ornithoid. I mean, a vratch."

"Sure," said Tony with a snort. "And I'm a wookie. Okay, I guess that's probably his picture and his apartment. But the picture's just a bunch of bushes, like the lady in the museum said. You're as crazy as—"

Tony stopped short, and Richard froze. Above their heads came the squeak of a window cranking open.

Without hesitating Tony plunged through the thorny bushes like a rhinoceros. Richard put his arms in front of his face and dashed after him to the bike rack.

"Hey, you little creeps!" called a man's voice, but they didn't look back.

For several blocks Richard and Tony just pedaled as hard as they could. Then, as they reached Mountain Avenue, Tony slowed down enough to look back at Richard. Tony was grinning widely.

Richard had thought he was too scared to be anything but scared, but now he pedaled slowly, too, and a smile started to spread over his face. Tony glanced back again, laughing, and Richard started to laugh, and then they were both laughing so hard that they had to pull over to the curb, leaning on their bikes. "Hey—you—little—creeps!" sputtered Tony.

The rest of the way home Richard felt good. They hadn't really done what they thought they were going to do—they didn't have any evidence to report to the SPCA, for instance—but Tony had been right about trying to make Dr. MacNary sweat. It made him feel better.

Richard's bike bumped over a storm drain grating, and the jolt sobered him. Just a minute. Why was he feeling so good? His hills were still in danger. In fact, now that Richard had seen the nature calendar picture, he knew that Dr. MacNary wouldn't stop until he had found that gray-green creature lurking in the sagebrush. Until he had found it—or ruined Richard's hills trying.

As they reached Tony's driveway, Mr. Heckman stopped cutting the lawn long enough to yell at Tony to come do his chores. Richard went home to check on Buck. The animal seemed to be waiting for Richard, sitting just inside the door of his room. With little gruff noises he led Richard to the edge of the rug, to a space of bare wooden floor beside the desk.

"What is it, Buck? Ants?" If ants were coming right into Richard's room, that would be very handy. In fact, he had toyed with the idea of dribbling a trail of honey from the patio to the wall outside his window and in the window to the floor. The only thing against it was that his mother might notice.

Then Richard focused on what Buck was showing him: deep scratches on the wooden floor. He gasped. "Buck! Why'd you have to do that? Bad dog!" Oh, brother. If Mom saw this, it would upset her a lot more than a trail of ants.

Frantically he glanced around the room for something, anything, to hide the scratches. Buck's floor pillow. Dragging the pillow across the room, Richard was relieved to see that it easily covered the scratches. There. Maybe he could find out how to repair the floor before Mom discovered the damage.

But why had Buck done it? Richard shook a forefinger at him. "Don't ever do that again—hear me?"

Buck hung his head. He looked almost discouraged, the way his shoulders slumped.

That afternoon Richard's father took him bowling. When they got home again, the phone was ringing as Mr. Hayes opened the kitchen door. Richard didn't pay any attention, since it seemed to be a call for his father, and he went straight to his room. It was time to take Buck outside.

But when he led Buck through the kitchen, his father said, "Some scientist wants to take a look at your dog."

6

Lessons from a Dog

Richard felt suddenly cold. "What scientist?"

"A Dr. MacNary," answered his father, pouring him-self a glass of apple juice. "Juice, Rich?"

"Why does he want to look at Buck?"

Mr. Hayes shrugged. "He said he's a cryp-to-zo-o-lo-gist—whew, that's a mouthful—and he's investigating leads on strange animals. He got our name from the animal shelter. He's going to come by Monday evening. He wanted to take Buck to his place for a couple of hours, but I told—"

"No!" Richard stared from Buck to his father in horror. "He can't! Dad, that guy does *experiments* on animals."

Mr. Hayes, looking astonished, put down his juice. "What makes you think that?"

"Because I saw him at the museum, that's what! I heard him say so."

Richard's father rubbed his forehead and squinted at his son as if he didn't know whether to believe him or not. "Hm. Well, anyway, I told this Dr. MacNary that

Buck wasn't well, and if he didn't seem a lot better by Monday, he'd have to look at him at our house.''

Richard swallowed. ''We can't let him look at Buck at all. This guy is bad. I *heard* him say he did experiments on animals. He might try to grab Buck and get away with him, or—'' It was no use. Dad was smiling.

''I know you think a lot of Buck, Rich, but I doubt that anyone else would commit a crime to get him. And I think you must have misunderstood what Dr. MacNary said, if it was the same person you overheard in the museum.'' He patted Richard's shoulder. ''Taking Buck out for his evening stroll? I must admit, you've been very responsible about taking care of your dog.''

That evening Richard's parents had some people over for dinner, so Richard ate early. When the guests rang the door bell, Richard snapped his fingers at Buck. He didn't want to stick around for ''This is our son, Richard'' and ''What grade are you in, dear?'' And maybe, tonight, ''What kind of doggie is that?''

''What do you want to do tonight?'' asked Richard as he led Buck down the hall. Remembering that he was supposed to brush Buck so that dog hair wouldn't get all over the house, Richard went to his closet and picked up the old hairbrush his mother had given him. But when he made a move toward Buck with the brush, the dog shifted away.

''Never mind, boy,'' said Richard. ''Your skin is probably sore, huh?'' He looked around the room for something else to talk about. ''Want to see my Revenge Drawer?'' He pulled open the middle drawer of his desk to show a pile of scratch paper, old printed forms his father brought home from the office. Richard riffled through the papers until he came to the pages, hidden in the middle of the pile, that he had drawn on. "If anyone makes me mad, I come home and draw a picture of them looking stupid. See?"

Buck stretched his neck forward, really interested in the pictures. Richard showed him one of Tony Heckman with his pants falling off, and one of the bossy lunch aide at school yelling with her mouth open so wide you could see her tonsils, and one of Mrs. VanNest in a flowery overblouse, looking as if she were made of sofa cushions. "I should give her that one for the paper, huh?"

Sitting down at his desk, Richard took out a fresh piece of scratch paper and a felt-tip pen, uncapped the pen, and stuck the cap on the other end. "Want to watch me draw?"

To Richard's surprise, Buck put his front paws up on the desk top, stretching his neck as if he really did want to watch Richard draw. He made low, creaky noises.

Richard felt a little uneasy. What was going on in Buck's mind? He drew a circle for a head, still talking as if Buck could understand him. "This is going to be that weird scientist in the museum, Dr. MacNary. Did I tell you about—Hey!"

With a quick movement, Buck had grabbed the pen in his teeth.

"No!" Grabbing back, Richard got hold of the cap, which came off in his hand, and then the end of the pen. "Drop it. Buck— *drop it.*" The felt tip was inside Buck's mouth. What if he swallowed it and poisoned himself? Buck leaned over the desk, the pen gripped tight.

"Okay, Buck, you asked for it." Richard rapped him sharply over the nose, at the same time yanking the pen from his jaws.

With a squawking yelp Buck let go and dropped to the floor. Richard examined the pen carefully, hoping that Buck hadn't bitten through to the ink part. No— there were only a few teeth marks in the plastic. Richard let his breath out and stood up. Silly of him, acting as if a dog would like to watch him draw. Buck must want to play tug-of-war.

It was easy to find an unmatched sock in his dresser drawer, even one with a hole in the toe so Mom couldn't complain about him using it for a dog toy. "Here, boy. Grab this!" Richard flipped the sock in front of Buck's face.

Buck looked at it as if to say, I see. An old sock.

"Hey, get it, boy." Dropping to his hands and knees, Richard gripped the top of the sock in his teeth, growling and shaking his head.

Buck turned his head away, as if he were embarrassed for Richard.

Richard sat up and spit out the sock. "I give up. I'm going to draw—you can do whatever you want." Sitting down at the desk again, he uncapped the felt pen and began sketching frizzy hair on the head.

Click, click. Out of the corner of his eye Richard saw two paws and a brown head appear beside his right elbow. He kept on drawing, but leaned forward with his right shoulder, in case Buck tried the same trick again.

"This is the evil scientist, Dr. MacNary," Richard

told Buck as he drew in bulging eyes. "I won't let him take you, no matter what Dad says."

As he drew MacNary's sport coat, Richard thought about the drawbacks of his black felt pen. He loved the way it glided over the paper, but it couldn't be erased. If he made a mistake, he had to start over. Another problem was no color. That was a big problem with a picture of MacNary, since the worst part of his looks was the color of his face. *Colors,* actually. Colors like that kind of luncheon meat you got at school sometimes, blotches of pink and purple.

As he drew a briefcase in the man's hand, it came back to Richard again, with a sickening rush, what Dr. MacNary was going to do to his hills. With Buck silently watching the point of the pen glide over the paper, it seemed natural to talk about it.

"He's going to take all these people up in the hills next week." Picking up a fresh piece of paper, Richard drew the hills behind his house, with Dr. MacNary leading a crowd of people over the ridge. "They'll trample down the brush, and look in all the canyons . . ." Concentrating on his drawing—it was hard to draw people climbing without making them look as if they were sticking sideways off the side of the hill— Richard was startled by a hoarse sound from Buck. Glancing over, he saw that the animal was trembling, staring at the picture. Almost as if something in Richard's drawing upset him.

It couldn't be that. Dogs couldn't understand pictures, of course. But it made Richard feel a little better to imagine that Buck, too, was horrified at the idea of all those people crawling over the hills. He probably would be, if he could understand. Buck had probably been hiding out in the hills himself.

"Don't worry." Richard patted his loose-skinned back. "Dr. MacNary isn't hunting for you. What he's really after is a vratch. Do you know what vratches are, Buck? They're sort of like little dinosaurs. Here, I'll show you."

Richard added to the picture a few heads and tails and little hands of vratches, hiding behind the bushes. Again Buck made a hoarse sound, not a growl but not really a bark, either.

"That's what Dr. MacNary *thinks*," explained Richard. To show that the vratches were only in MacNary's mind, he drew a circle around each one and connected them to the scientist's head with a string of bubbles. "And this is what he wants to happen." Pulling a third sheet of scratch paper from the drawer, he scribbled another cartoon of MacNary. This time he made the scientist smiling toothily and holding a cage with a vratch in it.

Raaac!

Richard hadn't even finished the long, thick tail sticking through the bars of the cage when Buck lunged across his arm and seized the pen. Before Richard could even think about grabbing it back, Buck was bounding around the room, uttering strange noises.

"Come back here!" Richard lunged after him, but Buck dodged and darted and ducked around the bedroom as swiftly as a lizard. And he was running on his hind legs.

This fact was so puzzling that Richard paused, panting, and leaned against the dresser. Buck couldn't be sick, after all, if he could run faster than Richard even on his hind legs. "What kind of dog *are* you? You must've gotten lost from a circus."

Buck paused, too, beside the desk, looking hard at Richard as if to make sure the boy had stopped chasing him. Then, with one powerful bound, he was up on the chair.

Richard moved closer to see what Buck was going to do, but he didn't try to grab the pen back. Chasing Buck had been the wrong thing to do, he realized now. When Buck took the pen the first time, and Richard grabbed it back, Buck must have thought it was some kind of a game. If Richard didn't do anything now, Buck would get bored and put the pen down.

Sure enough, Buck laid the pen down on the desk. Richard took a slow step closer, preparing to quietly take it away.

But Buck picked up the pen again, this time with the point sticking out of his mouth. Richard sighed and let his arm fall to his side. "All right, fool around all you want." He remembered something his father used to tell him. "I'm not going to play games with you."

Leaning over the desk, Buck put one elbow on each side of the paper. He bent his head and made a black mark at the top of the page, as if to test the pen.

And then he began to add little touches to Richard's picture of MacNary.

Richard held his breath. Buck is a very, very, very smart dog, he thought. I bet he's been on television. Look, he's imitating what I did.

Watching Buck make marks on Richard's picture, with his dark eyes so intent, reminded Richard of something he used to do when he was a little kid. He'd take a crayon in his fist and scribble in his coloring book, muttering, "Drawing, drawing, drawing."

Then Richard noticed that something was happening to his picture of Dr. MacNary. Instead of scribbling over it, Buck was adding a line here, shading there. It was looking more and more like a real person.

Richard's shoulder blades tingled, and he shivered. Wasn't this more than even a very, very, very smart dog could do? But Buck was doing it. Maybe he had been trained specially by an artist? But still . . .

Now Buck was touching up the sketch of the vratch in the cage. Under his pen strokes, the animal in the picture seemed to come alive. A gleam of desperation shone in its eyes.

"We should let it out," said Richard suddenly. Picking up a pencil, he leaned over Buck and drew an open door at one end of the cage.

Aaack. With a quick glance up at Richard, Buck traced over the pencil with black pen. Then he sketched the vratch first leaping from the cage, then bounding into the distance with its tail held high, then dwindling to a dot.

Richard let out his breath and drew it in again carefully, as if any sudden movement might turn Buck back into an ordinary dog. This is probably a dream, he warned himself. But then he answered himself, Okay—if it is, I'm going to get the most out of it.

For one thing, Richard thought, Buck knows something about vratches. He's seen them running, or he could never draw one like that. And he's probably friends with them, or why would he be upset at the idea of Dr. MacNary hunting them?

A great longing came over Richard, like the feeling he had staring at the animal hidden in MacNary's poster. "Show me," he said to Buck. Picking a blank piece of paper from the drawer, he put it in front of Buck. "Draw a nice big vratch."

But Buck set the pen down on the blank page. "Draw, Buck," said Richard very slowly and clearly. Buck only nudged the pen with his nose and looked at Richard. *You* show *me,* he seemed to be saying.

"All right. I'll start the picture." Richard began with the large hind legs, something like a kangaroo's—and jumped as Buck nipped his wrist. Not hard, just enough to jog his hand. "Cut that out, Buck." Well, it didn't matter. In fact, the jogged line looked more realistic, more three-dimensional. Richard started to attach an alligatorlike tail hanging down, and again Buck nipped his wrist. The line straightened, so that the creature on the page balanced on its tail like a kangaroo.

Resting his hand on the desk, Richard gazed at Buck. His heart began to pound. Buck was showing him how to draw.

Even if this *is* a dream, thought Richard, I'm lucky, lucky, lucky. This is the best dream I ever had. Don't wake up.

With his dry nose, Buck nudged Richard's right hand. Richard started to draw the vratch's back and head, but this time he let his hand glide loosely over the paper, ready to be guided by Buck. In a few minutes the page was filled with the creature from Dr. MacNary's nature calendar. But now Richard could see clearly the feathers covering its body except for its hands and its ostrich-like feet, and the crest standing up from its sleek head. The upper part of its body turned forward, so that its large, dark eyes gazed straight at Richard.

Richard bent over the desk, staring back. But Buck leaped off the chair with a hoarse bark. He began to dance from one side of Richard to the other, nipping and nudging as if he wanted him to do something.

"Hey, cut that out." Richard tried to dodge and stay at the desk, but Buck drove him out of his seat onto the middle of the carpet. "Leave me alone!"

He couldn't help laughing, though. It was funny, the way Buck looked with his front legs dangling, skipping around like a trained poodle. And it was funny the way he made Richard skip back and forth. Now and then Buck would stand back with his head on one side. It almost looked as if he was resting on his tail, like a person sitting on a camp stool.

Giving up, Richard let Buck lead him around and around the carpet. He began to imitate Buck's hops and turns, and shouted, "Braack!" when Buck uttered his grating bark. He even grabbed the old sock from the floor and tucked it into the back of his jeans waistband, for a tail. The faster they pranced around, the more carefree Richard felt, lighter and lighter as if he were going to rise off the carpet. Buck whacked his tail on the ground to beat time, and Richard stomped his feet. "Gratch!"

Richard's heart beat in time with the dance. He was floating, moving his arms and legs almost without trying. He might be someone else—someone who had lived a

hundred years ago, or five hundred. Leaping from side to side, he stretched his neck and snapped his jaws.

"Richard."

In the moment the door opened, Richard could only think, *No!*

He had never been so sorry to see his mother, although she looked pretty in her dinner party clothes. The scent of her perfume invaded the room. Richard's legs felt suddenly heavy, as if he were climbing out of a swimming pool.

"You're making such a racket!" She seemed to be more puzzled than angry—in fact, she was smiling. "We couldn't imagine what you were doing in here." She stooped over Buck. "Did poor Buck get all excited, running around your room? I think you worried him, Richard." Then she turned Richard around, peering at the back of his jeans. "What's this?"

Richard felt himself flush, and he yanked the sock out of his waistband. "We were just fooling around. Buck's okay." But he couldn't help noticing that Buck, down on all fours now, looked awkward and tired again. Hanging his head, he shuffled to his pillow and slumped down.

"Anyway, that's enough running around for tonight. Even from the living room, it sounded like some kind of wingding in here."

"But Mom—" As his mother paused, raising her eyebrows, Richard hesitated. Had it really happened or not? Even if it had, how could he describe it? "Buck isn't—I don't think Buck's really sick," he finally said.

"I guess he does seem a little better than yesterday." His mother wasn't looking at Buck, and her hand was on the doorknob. "Now I'm going to go serve the dessert, and you're going to get into your pajamas and read or something."

After his mother shut the door, Richard turned to look at Buck. Buck was stretched out on the floor pillow, his eyes shut. Was this the same animal that had been prancing around the room with Richard just a moment ago?

"Hey, Buck—want to dance?" Richard waited a second. Then stooping over Buck, he poked him gently in the ribs. Buck opened one eye and closed it again.

Sighing, Richard straightened and began to undress for bed. Buck was through fooling around, it looked like, and that was that. Maybe he would be rested and ready to play again tomorrow morning.

But anyway—what a dog! Who would have suspected, seeing Buck in the animal shelter, that he was some kind of dog genius? "Never was there such a dog," quoted Richard to himself. Richard's Buck.

7

Buck Is Missing

That night Richard's sleep was strange. It wasn't so much like real sleep as it was like the time he had his appendix out and spent the night in the hospital. He had lain floating in a sort of trance, dreaming and listening to what was going on around him, unable to tell the dreams from what was really happening.

First he half woke up, saw his room lit with moonlight, and turned over into sleep again. Later he seemed to hear the sound of paper rustling and a whispering *scratch, scratch, scratch*.

Richard sank far under the surface of sleep again, only to bob almost awake as his mattress jiggled. Then there was another sound: *ping, ping, ping*.

Then Richard drifted down again, dreaming that the Lagarto Grande hills were swarming with black ants, led by a red ant with a blotchy face. "Buck!" screamed Richard. "Here, Buck! Eat the ants." From far away he seemed to hear an answer: *vratch*. But Buck never came.

*   *   *

"Mom! Did you let Buck out?" Richard burst into the kitchen, holding Buck's empty collar.

Mrs. Hayes, pouring water into the coffee maker, yawned and blinked at him. "Buck? I thought he slept in your room."

"He's not there. And his collar fell off." Rushing out the door to the driveway, Richard stared across the street, down the street, up at the hills. Buck could be anywhere. "Bu-uck! Here, Buck! Mom, he doesn't have his license on."

"I'm sure he's right around the neighborhood," said his mother. "Probably raiding the VanNests' trash cans, and I'll hear about it later."

Hurrying back through the kitchen, Richard stuck his head into his parents' bedroom. "Dad. Did you get up early and let Buck out?"

His father opened his eyes, then closed them again, pulling the comforter up around his chin. "I certainly didn't get up early. I'm not going to get up now, either."

Slowly Richard walked back down the hall, remembering his strange dreams. Could he have gotten up in his sleep without knowing it and let Buck out himself? But however it happened, Buck was on the loose without a license . . . and Dr. MacNary would be pleased to run into him.

Knowing it was no use, Richard looked all around his room—under the bed, in the closet—again. Somehow it seemed to him that he was having to pay for his wonderful time—his dream?—for the time with Buck last night. Maybe Buck had left because he was afraid Richard knew too much and would sell him to the movies. But if

Buck were really as smart as Richard thought, wouldn't he understand he would be safer with Richard than running around the hills on his own?

A voice from the kitchen, Tony's voice, pulled Richard out of his miserable thoughts.

"Rich and me were going to ride bikes," explained Tony to Mrs. Hayes as Richard came into the kitchen. "Rich, want to ride bikes?" His eyes gleamed; he was ready for adventure.

"Rich has to have some breakfast before he goes anywhere." Mrs. Hayes handed her son a bakery bag. "Why don't you and Tony take muffins and juice out to the patio?"

Richard didn't think he felt like eating, but somehow having Tony around picked up his spirits. He ate a bran muffin. Tony bit into one, commented, "These taste like the kind that're supposed to make you healthy," finished it, and ate another. Then he asked, "Want to go spying again? I thought we could check the windows on the other side."

Richard shook his head, his throat tightening. "I have to look for Buck. Somehow he got out this morning, and he's gone. And Dr. MacNary wants to get hold of him. He called my Dad about that last night. What if he finds Buck?"

"Maybe Dr. MacNary *stole* him," suggested Tony.

"Shut up!" Richard glared at Tony, as if saying a terrible thing could make it true. Then he bit his lip. If he picked a fight with Tony, Tony wouldn't help him look for Buck. "It's just that I'm worried because I found out last night how smart Buck is. He must be worth a lot of money, so if someone else found him, they might not give him back.''

"Smart?" said Tony in a skeptical tone.

"Yeah. Not just regular tricks—he draws pictures, he dances around . . ." Richard's voice trailed off as he heard how ridiculous it sounded. When Richard thought to himself about Buck doing those things, it seemed real. But telling Tony about it gave him a feeling like trying to shove the wrong ends of two magnets together— they just forced themselves apart again.

Tony looked at Richard narrowly, as if he believed all this about as much as he had believed the story about dinosaurs in dog suits. But he only said, "I bet if I look around, I can figure out how Buck got out. Let's see your room."

"Okay." Richard jumped up, realizing that there was something in his room he had to check, anyway. If last night wasn't just a dream, the pictures would still be there.

The pictures lay on Richard's desk, black and white. He hadn't dreamed them. As Richard leaned on the desk, smiling with relief, Tony picked up the sketches and studied them. The drawing of Dr. MacNary made him guffaw at first, but then his face grew serious. He gave Richard a sizing-up look. "You can draw this good?"

Richard huffed his breath out impatiently. "Of course not. Buck drew them. I mean, I drew the first one and he fixed it up, and then he showed me how to draw the second one, the one of just the vratch. That's what I mean by *smart.*"

"A dinosaur with *feathers.*" Tony was looking at the

large picture of the vratch again. "You've got a weird imagination."

"And then he danced around on his hind legs just like a person," Richard went on doggedly. "Are you paying attention?" Remembering how *he* had danced, too, with a sock in the back of his jeans for a tail, Richard decided not to tell Tony that part.

With a scornful jerk of his wrist, Tony tossed the pictures onto the desk. "Don't give me that bull." He began to poke around under the bed in the closet and behind the desk. "Hey." He straightened up with a few pieces of paper in his hand. "Your dog drew some more pictures—they fell behind the desk." Tony's voice was sarcastic, but he shuffled through the pictures, looking at each one.

"Give me those!" Now Richard remembered a sound he had heard in his sleep—it was the rubbing of a felt-tip pen point on paper. "Buck left those for me."

The first picture showed a lumpy dog—Buck—in a tree-sheltered canyon, with several vratches around him. There was a picture of Richard (Richard could tell it was supposed to be him, although he didn't think his ears stuck out that much) walking into a building, and a picture of him coming out again with some long floppy strips. Bacon? There was a picture of Richard in the canyon, handing the strips to Buck. And the last picture showed Buck with several other awkward-looking dogs.

"I don't get it," said Tony. "You drew yourself pretty good, but what's that supposed to be?" He pointed to the strips.

"I told you, I didn't draw them. I think it's a message. I think Buck wants me to bring him some food, like bacon." But even as Richard said it, it didn't seem right.

Tony seemed to lose interest in the pictures. Turning from the desk, he gazed around the room, frowning. Richard followed his gaze up to the high window over the bed.

In the same moment that Richard saw the open flap of screen, the other sound from his sleep—*ping, ping, ping*—came back to him. "Wires!"

"That MacNary guy," said Tony grimly. "I was right! We go spying on him, but we don't even think about how he might go spying on you. Dumb. We let him get away with Buck!" He pointed to the cut screen. "He must have one of those long mechanical arms with grabbers on the end, and while you were asleep he just stuck it through the window, grabbed Buck, and made his getaway."

"No!" Richard jumped onto the bed, the sick feeling in his stomach coming back worse than ever. The hole in the screen was big enough for a medium-sized dog, all right. But on the window sill lay something Richard didn't expect: his Swiss Army knife, with the can opener sticking out.

Jumping onto the bed behind him, Tony picked up the knife. "Hey! What's going on here?" He looked at the can opener, looked at the screen, put down the knife, and looked at Richard with disgust. "You cut the screen yourself."

"I did not! Why don't you listen? Don't you get it?" Richard sputtered, caught his breath, and went on in a low tone. "Dr. MacNary didn't get Buck at all. *Buck* cut the screen. With my Swiss Army knife."

For a moment Tony stared at Richard with a cold stare, eyelids half shut. Then he drew up his fist so close to Richard's face that Richard found his eyes crossing, looking at the sticky orange juice smear on Tony's knuckles. "If you're fooling me about that mutt drawing and dancing, I'm going to punch your nose so hard, it'll point out the back of your head."

Richard had to bite his lip to keep from smiling at the idea. After all, he didn't want Tony to punch his nose. "I didn't make that up, I swear. See, I guess Buck took off to warn his friends the vratches that Dr. MacNary is coming hunting for them next week. And he left a message for me to bring him something."

Tony dropped his fist. Stepping off the bed, he went to the desk and squinted at the pictures again. Then he said, "When Buck danced around, what was that like?"

"How did he dance?" Richard's cheeks grew warm. "I don't know—just a dance. Like a folk dance, I guess."

"Well, show me."

Richard couldn't help thinking about how bad things would be for him at school if this got around. But he was too far into it to stop now. Holding his hands in front of him as if they were paws, he took a few steps forward—stamp, stamp—hop side to side, then forward again . . . Half shutting his eyes, he tried to picture Buck in front of him whirling with his tail out.

"Okay, that's enough." Tony's voice cut into his memory. "Don't you get it, Hayes?"

Opening his eyes wide, Richard frowned at the other boy. "What do you mean? You're the one who wouldn't believe my dog could do all this—"

"Jeez!" Tony blew the word out of his mouth. "Hayes—*this isn't any old dog.*"

"Of course he isn't a regular dog," said Richard, annoyed. "I could figure that out. That's why Dr. MacNary wanted to look at him. He must be a mutant, maybe from radioactive ore in the hills, or—"

Tony shook his head at Richard's unbelievable denseness. "Look." Picking up a pencil from the desk, he began to sketch a crude outline around the large picture of a vratch.

"Hey, cut that out!" Richard grabbed Tony's arm to keep him from spoiling the picture, but the other boy calmly jabbed his elbow into Richard's stomach.

Finishing the drawing with two floppy ears, he demanded, "Who's that? Don't you remember that whacko story you made up yourself about Buck?"

Richard stood there, staring at the clumsy dog outline Tony had drawn around the vratch. The two pictures, one around the other, seemed to take turns going in and out of focus. A dog—a vratch—a dog.

"Who's that, dumb-dumb?" repeated Tony.

Richard felt dumb, all right. He had been looking at Buck for two days, and he hadn't seen anything. He had ignored every hint. "That's a vratch . . . in a dog suit."

Taking the pencil from Tony, he used the eraser to rub out the dog outline. "That's Buck."

Now that the boys had figured out what Buck really was, everything else made more sense. The other "dogs" in Buck's last picture were vratches, too. And what Buck wanted Richard to bring him wasn't bacon. It was zippers, of course, so that all the vratches could have disguises. Luckily, Richard pointed out to Tony, they had money to buy zippers—the five dollars Dr. MacNary had tried to bribe them with.

"Zippers for little dinosaurs," grumbled Tony as their bikes coasted downhill toward the business section of Lagarto Grande. "We're crazy. We could rent a lot of good movies for five dollars." But Richard could tell by the way the other boy was swooping around the corners that he was enjoying himself.

Richard was pleased that he had remembered to count the vratches in the picture with Buck, so that they knew how many zippers to get. Nine. Then, as his bike skidded in a sandy place, he thought of something else. What *color* zippers? Should they all be brown, like Buck's dog suit?

No, he decided. A few should be black or white, so the vratches would look more like a real pack of dogs. He would get five brown, two white and two black.

The Sew-Sew Shoppe was next to the Koffee Kup on the main street of Lagarto Grande, and an aroma of coffee and bacon and pancakes drifted down the street to meet Richard and Tony. As the boys locked their bikes to a parking meter, Richard noticed a family with three little kids coming out of the coffee shop.

A lot of families went to the Koffee Kup for Sunday breakfast, thought Richard as he reached for the door of the Sew-Sew Shoppe. There came another family, two teenage girls and their father. The man paused to drop a letter in the mailbox beside the sewing store before he followed the girls into the coffee shop. Too bad Mom and Dad never wanted to—

Just a minute. *Sunday* morning. The thought struck

Richard in a different way as the locked door jerked his arm.

"Sunday," said Tony behind him in a tone of disgust. "I don't believe we did this." The boys stared at the hours lettered on the glass door: Mon.–Fri. 9–5. Sat. 10–3. Closed Sunday.

Richard groaned. He was sure this was the only place in Lagarto Grande that sold zippers.

"But hold on," said Tony, pointing to the back of the store. "There's a light on. And there's someone there."

The boys began tapping on the door and waving, until the woman at the far end of the store looked up and squinted at them across the yardage displays.

"Oh, boy," breathed Richard. "Maybe she'll sell us some zippers, even if it is closed."

But the woman only frowned, shook her head, and waved her shears to shoo them away.

Richard's heart sank. Tony made a horrible face, but now the woman's back was turned. "Who cares," he said. "I just had an idea—my folks might give us a ride to the mall this afternoon. We could go to Woolworth's. The trouble is, then they'd want to know what for and everything."

Richard brightened. "But we could tell them it was something else—something about the same size as zippers, you know—" He broke off as his eyes focused past Tony, at a man pushing open the screen door of the Koffee Kup.

A man with frizzy hair and a blotchy face.

As Dr. MacNary stood in front of the coffee shop for a moment, working his mouth as if he was getting the last of breakfast out of his teeth, Richard nudged Tony.

The other boy glanced over his shoulder, then without hesitating ducked behind the mailbox.

Richard crouched beside Tony, his heart pounding. What if Dr. MacNary had found out, at the animal shelter, that the police had picked Buck up here? And did he suspect anything more?

Peering around the blue bulk of the mailbox, Richard saw the cryptozoologist take a small notebook from his shirt pocket and study it. Then, to Richard's dismay, Dr. MacNary headed straight for the door of the Sew-Sew Shoppe. He glanced at the hours posted on the door, shaded his eyes to peer into the store, and began to tap and rattle the lock.

Richard's heart thudded even harder. What if Dr. MacNary guessed that Buck really had come here for the zippers?

When the woman came to the front of the store, she didn't look any more pleased to see Dr. MacNary than she had been to see Richard and Tony. "May I help you?" she asked, in a tone that said she would rather not.

"Mm." Dr. MacNary opened the door wider and began examining the lock. "Mm, yes. I have a scientific interest in the break-in."

"The break-in we had here on Monday?" The woman looked at him suspiciously, making clipping motions with her shears.

"Yes, the one involving the dog." Dr. MacNary finished looking at the lock and wrote something in his notebook. "That's what I wanted to interview you about. You see, I'm a zoologist specializing in extremely rare animals, and—"

"You want to interview me?" The woman sounded surprised and pleased.

Cramped from crouching behind the mailbox, Richard watched Dr. MacNary lean impressively toward the woman. "Yes. I have reason to think that the dog they found here after the burglary may be a crossbreed with—" He broke off, as if he wondered whether she could be trusted with important information. "Did it occur to you that the burglar might have been the dog himself?"

The pleased expression disappeared from the woman's face. "Ah—no, not exactly." Her lips twitched. "You know, it's been nice talking with you, but I'm terribly busy today, so . . ."

Drawing back, Dr. MacNary narrowed his eyes at the saleswoman. "Mounce has been here! Poisoning your mind against me."

"Mounce?" The woman looked confused. "One of the policemen?"

"Heh," laughed MacNary scornfully. "No. Mounce, the so-called desert ornithologist. Mounce is out to ruin me, in case you didn't know." The saleswoman didn't look as if she knew, even now, but Dr. MacNary went on. "I'd like to place a notice in the window." He pulled a large card from his briefcase. "A notice about my class in cryptozoology, which focuses on the search for a heretofore undiscovered species, living in the Lagarto Grande hills."

"I suppose so." The woman sounded more baffled than ever. "I'll get some tape. When does the class start?"

"I'm kicking it off with an exploratory search the day after tomorrow," said Dr. MacNary. "Timing is very important, don't you agree? I have to make my move now, before Mounce succeeds in undermining me.''

Looking at Tony with dismay, Richard put his hands on the side of the mailbox to steady himself. Dr. MacNary had jumped his schedule ahead a whole week. MacNary's words echoed in his ears: *The day after tomorrow.*

8

Puppy Suits

"That sure was a big fat waste of time," remarked Tony as they pushed their bikes up his driveway. "Well, at least we still have five dollars."

"And it's just as well we didn't spend it on zippers," said Richard. "Buck couldn't make enough disguises by the day after tomorrow. But we've still got to hike up to his canyon. We've got to warn him."

Tony nodded. "Want to have lunch at my house first?"

"Yeah. I'll go tell my mom."

Richard rolled down Tony's driveway, across the street, and up his own driveway. He found his mother sitting in a lounge chair on the patio, reading the Sunday paper. "Fine, if it's all right with Tony's mother," she answered his question. "By the way, Mrs. VanNest was so pleased with the pictures you drew for her."

"The what?"

"You know, you said you were going to draw some new pictures for Mrs. VanNest to put in the paper. You left them on your desk. She oohed and ahed over all of them, but she took the one of the funny imaginary animal." His mother smiled at him. "She said it'll be in this week's *Grande View*."

Richard felt cold. "You let her take that picture? To put in—in the paper?"

"What's the matter?" Mrs. Hayes looked surprised. "Don't worry, she'll give the picture back after the paper comes out. The day after tomorrow."

Choking back an outburst, Richard nodded. It had given him an awful shock to imagine the vratch picture in every copy of the *Grande View*, the day of Dr. MacNary's search of the hills. Thousands of people would see his drawing, including Mrs. VanNest and all the others following MacNary on the hunt. But maybe they wouldn't make the connection. And the more of a fuss Richard made about losing the picture, the more his mother, and maybe Mrs. VanNest, might wonder just what was so special about it.

Still, the idea of the vratch picture in the paper made him more worried than ever. Back in Tony's driveway, he said, "If we could get zippers this afternoon, maybe the vratches could make a couple of disguises, anyway."

Tony snickered. "Hey, I had a good idea for how to get zippers. You could—cut them out of your jeans!" He clutched his waistband, pretending to hold his jeans together, and toddled a few steps. "I can explain, Mom," he whined in a voice that was supposed to be Richard's. "I had to give my zippers to these little dinosaurs—they needed them real bad—"

"Very funny," grunted Richard.

"Anyway," Tony went on in a normal voice, "the zippers wouldn't do them any good. My mom's been making puppy costumes for the nursery school show, and it's taking her forever. And *she* has a sewing machine."

"Puppy costumes?" An idea burst in Richard's head. "For the nursery school kids? Can I see them?"

Tony stared at Richard blankly. "You want to see—" Then his eyebrows lifted as he caught on. "Come *on.*"

Richard followed Tony through the house to a bedroom, where Tony's little sister Kimmy was standing on a chair with her arms out. Mrs. Heckman, bending over her daughter, looked up from the furry suit she was folding and pinning.

"Hi, Tony, hi, Richard!" The little girl wiggled her fingers and shook her blond curls. "Richard, this is my costume for the dance at my school." She gave a hop on the chair.

"Hold still, Kimmy." Frowning, her mother paused to push up the sleeves of her sweatshirt. "Tony, do you mind? Kimmy can't concentrate with anyone else around."

"You can come to see the dance at my school," the little girl said kindly to Richard. "Everybody can come."

Richard said nothing. He couldn't take his eyes off Kimmy's costume. It was made of brown fake fur, with a zipper up the front and a hood with two floppy black ears. The thick black tail, which looked like it was stuffed with cotton, lay on the bedspread.

"Wowee, we can come to the dance," said Tony. He gave Richard a meaningful glance, rolling his eyes.

"Hold *still,* Kimberly," said Mrs. Heckman. "I don't want to stick you with a pin. Look, Tony, why don't you boys go make yourselves some lunch. Please don't

stand around here getting Kimmy excited. I have eight more of these to finish, and I want to sew all the tails on tonight.''

"Sorry," said Tony cheerfully. "Come on, Rich."

Richard trailed after him, dazed, into the Heckmans' kitchen. *Eight more of these.* "Your mom has *all* the puppy costumes?''

Tony nodded. "Nine puppy-dog costumes! Now, who do we know who could use something like that?'' He took jars of peanut butter and jelly from the cupboard. "If we skipped school on Tuesday,'' he said with a thoughtful squint, "we could get the costumes and take them to Buck that afternoon. Dr. MacNary probably wouldn't get up to the canyon before that. We could pretend we were—''

"No," said Richard, climbing onto a stool at the breakfast bar. "That would be too late. The vratches don't just need disguises. They have to *leave.*''

"What do you mean, leave? Where're they going to go—Disneyland?''

Richard watched Tony unscrew the jar lids and spread two slices of bread with peanut butter, two with jelly. "They've got to go somewhere where nobody will bother them. Like—remember when we studied ecology, Mr. Hassler said there was a wilderness preserve on the other side of the desert? The Turtle Mountains? That's where they should go. And they should start tonight.''

"Uh-uh." Slapping the sandwiches together as if he were laying tiles, Tony shook his head. "I can see why you thought it was a great idea, but it's not going to work out.''

"Yes it is! What do you mean?" Richard crouched

on the bar stool like a hungry mountain lion. "If we take the costumes up there this afternoon, Buck and the rest of them can leave tonight. By the time Dr. MacNary gets up there, the day after tomorrow, they'll be all the way to the Turtle Mountains, I bet." Seeing in his mind MacNary's crew rooting about in the hills, Richard bit his lip. MacNary, thinking the vratch must be there somewhere, would tear the hills apart sagebrush clump by clump.

Tony put each sandwich on a paper napkin and set them on the bar with a bag of potato chips. "We *can't* take the costumes up there this afternoon. The day after tomorrow is when the nursery school kids are going to do the Dance of the Puppy Dogs. Kimmy would throw a fit. My mom would kill me." Tony smiled lopsidedly. "My dad would skin me alive."

"Look, okay," said Richard, hardly paying attention. "Your mom and Kimmy would probably be a little upset if they found out the costumes are missing. So would *my* mom, as a matter of fact—she's Kimmy's teacher, remember? But they won't be put in cages and experimented on, like the vratches will be if Dr. MacNary gets hold of them. And don't worry about the costumes, because—" Richard had to pause for a minute. Why shouldn't Tony be worried about the costumes? "Don't worry, because I'll tell Buck to bring them back tomorrow, after the vratches get to the wilderness. I'll draw him a picture message."

"Huh," said Tony. He pulled his sandwich apart, rubbed the jelly into the corners, and closed it again. "I don't know. Why should Buck care what happens to me, or anything about my sister's nursery school, as long as the vratches get away?''

"He *would* care," said Richard. "He'd never let anyone down. He's not that kind of person."

Tony bit into his sandwich. "Person?" he asked stickily.

But Richard was in a trance, seeing Buck's dark eyes on him. He remembered how Buck had watched him, how Buck had guided Richard's hand to draw the picture of the vratch, how he had led Richard in the dance. Richard's heart filled with a joyful longing. He opened his mouth, sighed, and closed it. Explaining what Buck was like was as hard as talking under water. "So as long as we ask him to bring the costumes back . . . I swear!"

"Wow." Tony pretended his head was reeling from Richard's passionate speech. Pulling open the bag of chips, he gave Richard a half grin. "Sounds like things got turned around—you're talking like Buck owns you, and you're the dog."

"Oh, jeez. That's not what I mean." But maybe it was, thought Richard. His face grew warm, and he concentrated on folding his sandwich exactly in half. "Anyway . . . Buck needs the costumes *desperately*. How would you like it if you were in a cage, and you saw Dr. MacNary get out his experiment kit to start on you?"

Putting down his sandwich, Tony looked at Richard with a completely serious face. His mouth was straight for once, and his eyes round. "Yeah. We've got to stop that slime." He jerked his head in a nod. "Okay. We'll do it."

It wasn't that simple, though. Tony said his parents were going to go to a furniture sale that afternoon, but Tony's mother kept on working and working on the costumes. "I guess I could write the message while we're waiting," said Richard. "Have you got a piece of paper?"

In his book bag Tony found a blank piece of paper—blank except for his name, the date, *Social Studies,* and a red *F* at the top. "Use the other side of this—I wasn't going to show it to my dad, anyway."

Kneeling on Tony's bedroom floor, Richard drew frames like a comic strip, explaining to Buck why he should leave the Lagarto Grande hills immediately. "I wish he could read," muttered Richard, nibbling the end of the pen. It was easy to draw Dr. MacNary and his gang chasing vratches, but not so easy to draw "the day after tomorrow."

"Do you think he's going to get the idea from two suns coming up and going down?" asked Tony doubtfully. He was on his hands and knees, looking over Richard's shoulder. "They'd have to be as smart as dolphins."

"Dolphins!" Richard jerked his head up from his work, shocked. "They're smarter than *you,* if you think they're like dolphins. They're so smart, the Indians thought they were the Great Lizard Spirit."

Finally Richard was satisfied that his picture message was at least as clear as Buck's had been. "Except for the part about the wilderness preserve," he said with a frown. "I don't know exactly where it is. I wish I could give him a map."

"We can!" Tony bounced up. "I bet there's one in the Jeep."

Sure enough, in the pocket on the inside of the door of the Heckmans' Jeep, Tony found a map of Lagarto Grande County, one that showed the Turtle Mountain Wilderness Preserve on its southeastern edge. The boys stood in the clear sunshine on the driveway, admiring the map.

"I can draw pictures on this," said Richard, "to make sure they know where they're starting from. I'll put in my house here, and the vratches in the canyon—"

"How can you tell where the canyon is?" interrupted Tony. "All the map shows for hills and canyons is darker brown and lighter brown."

Richard admitted that he would have to guess. "They know where they are, anyway. And I'll put in arrows," he went on, "leading to the wilderness."

Startled by the front door clicking open, Tony quickly folded up the map and jammed it into his back pocket. Kimmy came dancing down the walk in front of Mr. and Mrs. Heckman. "We're going to go buy furniture!" she chirped. "I'm going to help pick out a sofa, a sofa with a fold-out bed. Me and Heather can sleep in it when she sleeps over."

Tony smiled a falsely loving smile at his little sister as she climbed into the Jeep. "That's nice. I'll wait until you get in, and then I'll fold you up in it."

Starting the engine, Mr. Heckman rested one brawny arm on the window and leaned out toward Tony. "Behave yourself while we're gone, wise guy. You get into trouble, I'll tan your hiney when I get back."

As soon as the Jeep had disappeared around the first

curve of Vista Drive, Richard and Tony ran inside. Richard drew on the map with a green felt-tip pen, while Tony stuffed the nine puppy costumes and nine tails into two plastic trash bags.

The sun, still high but over the western hills by now, threw sharp shadows onto the rising trail in front of the boys. At first Tony kept up a chatter behind Richard about how mad MacNary was going to be, and whether they should join the hunt for the vratches just to see his face, and maybe lead him in the wrong direction. Then his words came out between panting, as the trail sloped more steeply. And then Richard didn't hear anything except his loud breathing until they reached the top of the first hill.

The boys paused, put down their bags and looked back, leaning with their hands on their knees. Raising his head, Tony shaded his eyes to gaze over the valley. "All *right*. You can see everything from up here."

Richard nodded, feeling the breeze dry his sweaty forehead. "Didn't you come up this far before?"

Tony turned and picked up his bag again. "Uh-uh. There weren't any bike trails up here."

Farther on, peering into an oak-overgrown canyon, Tony remarked, "We could have an awesome fort up here."

"Yeah, we could," agreed Richard but without much enthusiasm. He didn't want to think about going into the hills after Tuesday. There would be stakes with red flags all over, and footprints in the bare dusty patches, and crushed dents in the brush, and broken yucca stalks. He could even imagine MacNary hiring a bulldozer to scrape off all the hiding places.

"Whew." Ahead of Richard on the trail now, Tony paused, shifting the bag to his other shoulder. "Are we getting close?"

Richard grinned. "Almost there." He thought of what Tony had said before about Richard being Buck's dog. It was as if Buck had commanded, "Richard, fetch. Fetch zippers." But Richard didn't feel insulted. It made him feel proud, helping Buck. "See that big bush with reddish leaves up ahead?" he asked Tony. "The next canyon is Canyon Vratch."

A minute later, looking down the steep side of the canyon toward its oak-hidden floor, Richard wondered what to do. "I don't see any trail down."

Tony shrugged. "Let's just crash down through the brush. I want to see a vratch."

"No, *no.*" Richard was sure that was a bad idea. "When Dr. MacNary gets up here, we don't want to leave him any clues. A new trail down to the canyon would lead him right to where the vratches lived."

Turning around to look back the way they had come, Richard felt an idea forming in his mind. "Hey, you know that big bush I showed you? I bet one of the vratches keeps a lookout there." He imagined Buck or one of his friends crouched under the branches, doodling a picture in the dirt with one clawed finger.

"Oh, yeah? Let's go look." Before Richard could stop him, Tony jogged down the trail and was peering under the bush.

"You idiot!" whispered Richard, but of course the hiding place under the bush was empty. "He must have run down to the canyon as soon as he heard us coming in the first place. You know what? I think we should

93

leave the costumes right here. They'll find them after we leave.''

So the boys pushed the dark green plastic bags under the bush. Then they stood for a moment at the top of the canyon. The wind lifted a sound up from the scrubby oaks. *Vratch.*

Richard smiled at Tony. "Buck," he whispered.

Tony's eyes widened. But all he said was, "Just sounds like a crow or something to me."

The boys stood still again, listening. Once more they heard a rasping voice: *vratch, vraatch.*

"I guess that means, 'Thanks, guys,' " remarked Tony. "All I can say is, he better get those puppy suits back here by tomorrow night."

"He'll do it," said Richard. "I drew him a picture."

9

The Surprise Exhibit

"Richard," said his mother the minute he walked into the kitchen. He gulped at her stern tone—had the theft of the puppy costumes been discovered already? But she went on, "I found something in your room just now that upset me. Please come here and explain how this happened."

Richard followed her down the hall. Something in his room? Had she found his revenge pictures? But why would they upset her? He hadn't drawn one of her or Dad.

In Richard's room Mrs. Hayes picked up the dust mop leaning against the desk and pointed to the floor. "How did *that* get there, please tell me?"

"Oh my gosh." It was the scratches Buck had made on the wooden floor—a picture of a vratch, Richard saw now. "I'm sorry, Mom. Buck did it yesterday, and I was going to fix it, but then I—"

"Buck!" She snorted. "Please, Richard, you're too old to blame the dog for scribbling pictures on the floor. I *thought* you were too old to scribble pictures on the floor, as far as that goes."

Richard hung his head, staring at the vratch scratched on the polished boards. What a dummy he was. Of course Mom wouldn't believe that Buck had drawn the picture on the floor. Especially since it was just like the other picture she thought Richard had drawn, the one Mrs. VanNest had taken.

His mother gave a deep sigh. "I don't know what got into you. Unless you're mixed up because you're worried about Buck. Did you and Tony go looking for him today?"

Richard hesitated, then nodded. It was sort of true—he *had* hoped he would see Buck again when he and Tony dropped off the costumes.

At dinner Richard was silent, wondering whether Tony was right, and they should skip school on Tuesday and try to keep MacNary off the track.

"You're worried about Buck, aren't you, son?"

Richard looked up from his plate in surprise. His father went on quickly, as if he didn't want to upset Richard by talking about it too much. "Listen, if he doesn't show up by tomorrow night, Tuesday morning we'll call the animal shelter and all the vets around Lagarto Grande. I'd call them tomorrow, except they'll be closed for the holiday."

"Okay," said Richard, trying not to feel guilty. After all, he *was* worried about Buck. What would Dr. MacNary find in the vratches' canyon? Nothing, he hoped, dragging the skin of his stuffed green pepper around his plate. After all, the vratches must be very good at covering their traces, or they would have been discovered a long time ago.

"Eat the pepper skin, too, Rich," said his mother.

"It would have tasted a lot better if you'd eaten it with the stuffing, but now—" The doorbell interrupted her.

"I'll get that." Richard's father pushed back his chair. "Probably someone selling magazines."

But it was Mr. and Mrs. VanNest. Mr. VanNest, a balding man with droopy eyes, stepped back out the door as soon as he saw the Hayeses were eating. "Come on, Gloria, we don't want to barge in on their dinner." He almost tripped over Snowball, wheezing behind him.

"I'm so sorry!" exclaimed Mrs. VanNest. "Please sit down, folks, and go right on eating. I won't take half a minute." She leaned comfortably against the counter, patting her hair. "I must look wild—Harry and Snowball and I have been for our evening walk, and there's quite a wind blowing up the canyon. Then I thought of Richard as we came by your house, and I said to Harry, I'll just stop in and settle it now. You see, the *Grande View* has assigned me to cover the Cryptozoological Association conference in Riverside tomorrow, and I'll be gone all day."

"Oh, really?" asked Mrs. Hayes politely. "That should be interesting."

"Fascinating!" Mrs. VanNest's cheeks were pink. "Dr. MacNary showed me the program. There's a talk on the Abominable Snowman, and a panel discussion about the giant octopus of the Mariana Trench, and I don't know what-all."

"Oh, really?" asked Mr. Hayes.

"Gloria," said Mr. VanNest from the doorway. "Get to the point and let these poor folks go back to their dinner." At the word "dinner," Snowball licked her chops and whined.

"I'm so sorry," said Mrs. VanNest again. "The point is that at the end of his talk, Dr. MacNary is going to reveal a surprise exhibit. Something that will get the whole Association behind him and shut up his enemy Dr. Mounce once and for all. After tomorrow, he should have hundreds of trained zoologists, besides the amateurs like me"—she laughed modestly—"who've already signed up for his course, to search the hills."

Richard stared at her in horror. *Hundreds of trained zoologists.* The vratches' chances of escape, which had seemed pretty good a minute ago, were suddenly dim. The idea of Mrs. VanNest and people like her, huffing and puffing up the trails in the hills, hadn't seemed very scary. Mrs. VanNest would be so busy chatting with the other ladies that she would hardly notice a brontosaurus if it reared up in front of her, let alone a vratch in disguise.

But the scientists wouldn't be huffing and chatting—they would be *looking.* If trained zoologists saw dozens of footprints from puppy-dog costumes, they would be suspicious.

"And what do you think, Richard?" Mrs. VanNest smiled at him, her head on one side. "Dr. MacNary has chosen *your* drawing to use in his presentation tomorrow!"

Richard sat paralyzed in his chair, but Mrs. VanNest must have thought he was overcome with joy. "Of course, his surprise exhibit is the main thing, but he felt that a lifelike drawing of the ornithoid would help whip up enthusiasm."

"You mean he thinks the creature he's hunting for actually looks like Richard's picture?" asked Mrs. Hayes. "But how did Dr. MacNary get hold of that picture?"

"Not the actual picture—I made a photocopy for him. You see, when Dr. MacNary dropped by the *Grande View* office this afternoon—Harry doesn't like me to work on Sundays, but the school page *must* go in every week—*some*body has to do it—"

"*Gloria,*" said Mr. VanNest. "The point of our stopping by and interrupting the Hayeses' dinner was Snowball."

"Oh, yes. Silly me!" Rolling her eyes upward and pinching her chin between thumb and forefinger, Mrs. VanNest gave a little laugh. "The point is, I'll be gone until six or seven, and Harry's going up to Santa Barbara to visit his mother, so Snowball will be alone all day."

At "Snowball," the dog whimpered and wagged her tail. "Relax, sweetheart," ordered Mr. VanNest.

Richard saw his father take a sip of water to hide his smile. His mother said, "Would you like me to go over and look in on Snowball?"

"Oh, no, Suzy, I wouldn't dream of imposing on you. I was hoping I could hire Richard to give Snowball her dinner." She smiled at Richard. "And I know you'd give her a friendly pat, too."

"Sure," said Richard, still dazed.

"Why doesn't Richard come over in the morning before you leave," suggested Mrs. Hayes. "Then you can show him where you keep the dog food and whatever."

After the VanNests had left, Richard's father grinned. "I'm glad Gloria didn't stay half a minute and interrupt our dinner."

Richard's mother laughed, helping herself to another

stuffed pepper. "What amazes me is how impressed she is with this Dr. MacNary. I think he's getting away with a lot, asking people to pay to take his cryptozoology class, which is nothing but doing his fieldwork for him. He must be quite a con artist." Her glance fell on Richard's plate. "Richard, come on—eat the pepper skin."

"I'm not hungry, Mom. Can I go over to Tony's? We—we were going to watch a movie tonight."

Naturally his mother made him finish the pepper skin first. "I knew there was some way to get you to do that," she remarked as he gulped it down in three bites. "You can stay at Tony's until ten, if that's all right with his mother."

Under the yellow light of the lantern outside the Heckmans' door, Richard whispered the latest development to Tony. "If we could just find Dr. Mounce," he finished. "He's the only person who might want to talk the other scientists out of helping Dr. MacNary."

"Talk," said Tony. "Is that all you can think of? Anyway, that Mounce guy is probably just as big a fruitcake as Dr. MacNary. What we should do is—go to the offense!" He smacked a fist into his palm. "That's what my dad always says—he used to play football. 'Go to the offense!' "

"Sure, that sounds great," said Richard grumpily. "Like for instance, what does that mean?"

"I'll tell you what it means," said Tony. "It means, go find out what MacNary's big surprise is."

"Oh." Richard felt stupid for not thinking of that, himself. "You mean, right now?"

"Yeah," said Tony with a mocking grin. He opened

the door and stuck his head in. "Mom—I'm going to Richard's for a couple of hours, okay?"

Down at the Lagarto Palms Apartments, Richard thought that it was much easier to spy in the nighttime, with all the shadows to hide in, than in the daytime. And there was a soccer game going on in the park across the street, so Richard felt that no one would notice a couple of extra boys on bikes. They leaned their bikes against the chain-link fence around the ball field, and trotted across the street.

Floodlights shone on the entrance to the Lagarto Palms, but not on the bushes under the windows. The boys slipped into the thick shrubbery once more. Richard's heart beat faster, and he wondered what Dr. MacNary would do to a boy he caught spying. He remembered how swollen MacNary's face had looked in the museum when he told them, "No one is going to stop me from getting my hands on the ornithoid."

As Tony gave him a leg up to Dr. MacNary's window, Richard whispered, "What if he happens to raise the shade just when I'm looking in?"

Tony sighed. "You worry about everything. Why would he do that? Anyway, the worst thing he can do is call the cops."

"Call the cops—great," groaned Richard. But he was ashamed of himself for having the jitters. Nerves of steel, he told himself as he braced his elbows on the window ledge. He should have muscles of iron, nerves of steel.

It *was* easier to spy at night—with the light inside and the dark outside, he could see right through the bamboo shade. There was the Formica table in the little kitchen. And—

Richard stopped breathing. Dr. MacNary, wearing a shirt and tie but no slacks, sat at the table. Richard swallowed a giggle at the sight of the scientist's polka-dot underwear. Then he recognized the two white things Dr. MacNary was working with, and the giggle faded into a shudder. Those were skulls.

The skulls were about the same size, but one was rounded with a large beak. The beak was propped open with wooden skewers, and a drill lay near it on the table. The other skull was flat with a long toothy jaw. As Richard watched, the cryptozoologist picked up a small pair of pliers, pulled a sharp tooth from the jaw, dabbed its root with a bottle of Elmer's glue, and stuck it precisely into one of the sockets along the edge of the beak. A gentle smile curved his purplish lips.

Now Richard noticed the hand-lettered cardboard sign, folded to stand up, at the end of the table. *Present-day Ornithoid,* it read.

This was it, then. The surprise exhibit for the cryptozoology conference tomorrow. Richard imagined an auditorium full of scientists staring excitedly at the skull, jumping up to charge into the Lagarto Grande hills and track down that animal.

"That's long enough, Hayes." Tony jiggled the foot in his hands. "Let me see."

Jumping carefully down, Richard held out his interlocked hands for Tony. "Boy, oh boy, oh boy. Wait till you see this."

Tony only stayed up at the window for a moment. First Richard heard him let out his breath, as if in surprise. Then he was silent. And then he moved himself away from the window and jumped down, not-so-accidentally kicking Richard in the chest.

"Watch it!" said Richard. "Hey, did you see what he's doing? He's faking the skull. That means—"

"That means we're playing games here," said Tony in a dangerous voice. "Pretend animals. That means I stole my sister's puppy costumes and dumped them in the hills for nothing."

Backing away from Tony's fists, through the thorns, Richard tried to argue. "It's not a game! Don't you get it? It's just Dr. MacNary who's—" As Tony punched him in the arm, Richard turned and plunged through the bushes.

He ran under the palms, right through the spotlight, as if they had never thought of trying to slink around without being seen. With Tony's sneakers pounding after him, he jumped on his bike and started pedaling as hard as if Dr. MacNary had really called the police.

Richard pedaled past the stores and gas stations, then up the long straight slope of Lagarto Grande Boulevard. Under a streetlight, into the shadow again, streetlight, shadow, light-shadow-light. He could hear the wheels of Tony's bike whirring behind him, and once the other boy panted, "You're going to get it, Hayes!"

Then, as he reached Mountain Avenue, Richard realized that he couldn't hear Tony's bike behind him anymore. He didn't stop, but pedaled more slowly, catching his breath and giving his cramped leg muscles a chance to straighten out.

Richard couldn't believe what had happened. How could Tony think Richard would try to fool him, making up all this stuff about vratches? Tony must think Richard was . . . was a person like Dr. MacNary. That hurt more than Richard's arm, which ached where Tony had punched him.

Why did Tony have to fly off the handle like that? Simmer down, you dummy! Richard wanted to shout at him. Just listen a minute. This is our chance to make Dr. MacNary sweat!

More than sweat. If the scientists knew Dr. MacNary had faked the skull, they'd react just like Tony had. They'd never believe there might be ornithoids in the hills. No one would follow MacNary on the hunt—not the scientists, not even the ladies like Mrs. VanNest.

Telling people was going to be a problem, though. If Richard and Tony were scientists, they could go to that meeting tomorrow and stand up and tell everyone what a fake Dr. MacNary was. But they were only kids, so no one would listen to them. They didn't even have proof, like a photograph of MacNary working on the skulls.

Richard frowned at the clump of eucalyptus trees ahead, marking the corner of Vista Drive. Of course there was *one* person who would want to believe that Dr. MacNary was a fake. One person who could help Richard and the vratches, if Richard could only find him: Dr. Mounce.

Richard pumped his bike uphill, his head down. Mounce probably didn't live in Lagarto Grande. Mrs. VanNest had said the cryptozoologists were coming from all over the Southwest for this conference tomorrow.

Richard's bike jolted over the edge of his driveway, and he still didn't have any ideas about how to find Dr. Mounce. I can look in the phone book, anyway, he thought without much hope. Hearing the click of bicycle gears and the sound of panting a little way down the street, he put his bike in the garage and hurried inside.

As Richard was opening the refrigerator for some juice, the phone rang. A woman's voice, not loud but with a frightening sort of held-back tone, spoke in his ear. "Richard. Tell Tony to come home right away. We want to—Never mind, here he is."

Richard hung up the phone with a sinking feeling in his stomach. Why did Tony's mother have to find out tonight? She didn't really need the puppy costumes right now, although Richard remembered she had said something about sewing on the tails. If things had gone according to Tony and Richard's plan, they would have hiked into the hills tomorrow to collect the costumes, which Buck would have returned by that time. Then the boys would have sneaked the costumes back to Mrs. Heckman's closet without anyone getting upset.

Or punished. Richard felt a pang of guilt. Mr. Heckman's words to Tony that afternoon came back to him: "You get into trouble, I'll tan your hiney." And the worst thing was that Tony thought it was all for nothing, that Richard had gotten him into bad trouble just for a game.

Meanwhile, what was Richard going to do? He didn't even have Tony to help him, and he had to figure out a way to find Dr. Mounce before the conference.

Frowning, Richard focused his gaze on a yellow reminder slip his mother had stuck on the refrigerator door: *Mon. a.m.: Rich to VanNests'*.

To VanNests'. Yes! Richard sat up straight. That's what he should do—not tomorrow a.m., but right now.

Get Mrs. VanNest to take him to the Cryptozoological Association conference! Because Dr. Mounce would have to be there.

Mrs. VanNest didn't answer the tapping of the woodpecker knocker on her door right away. Richard shivered, hugging himself in the cool night air.

"Who is it?" The door was still closed, but a little window above the woodpecker had opened. "Richard! What do you want at this time of evening?"

"I'm sorry to bother you—I have to talk to you about tomorrow." His teeth chattered, and he jumped in place to warm himself up.

Opening the door, Mrs. VanNest looked at him sternly. "Richard, we agreed that you would come over tomorrow morning, not tonight." She was wearing a bathrobe with a wide ruffle around the neck, and her hair was covered with a puffy flowered cap. "Never mind, I can't be too put out. It *was* responsible of you to remember you had to come talk to me about Snowball. But you should have worn a jacket, you'll catch cold."

"Snowball?" Richard was puzzled, because he wasn't going to talk to her about Snowball at all. Then he remembered: she had stopped by at dinner to ask him to feed the dog. "Oh. Mrs. VanNest, would you mind if my mother fed Snowball tomorrow, instead? Because I really want to go to the conference with you. Would you please let me come? It would be really exciting. It would be so nice of you if you would let me come."

It took a few minutes to convince Mrs. VanNest that Richard was really, really interested in cryptozoology and would be horribly disappointed if he didn't get to go to the conference and hear all the talks. "They'll be speaking in very scientific terms, you know,'' she said doubtfully. ''I'm not sure I'm going to understand every word myself.''

Also, she wasn't sure she wanted Richard's mother to feed Snowball. ''Suzy is a sweetheart—of course she'd do it. But I wouldn't impose on her for anything.''

Finally they agreed that Richard would go home and ask his parents if he could go. If he could go, he would be ready tomorrow at nine o'clock sharp, dressed in his best clothes. Richard didn't like that part, but Mrs. VanNest refused to take him to the conference in jeans.

And Richard had to get to the conference.

10

Looking for Dr. Mounce

That night Richard fell asleep instantly, like falling down a well, worn out from all the hiking and biking of the day. But later he woke up just as suddenly, feeling sure that everything was going wrong.

Richard glanced at the clock on his dresser: only 11:06. Then he turned over. But instead of going back to sleep, he began to feel stung and itchy. It was from all the thorns that had scratched him earlier that evening, as he plunged through the bushes to escape Tony's fists.

Thorny thoughts seemed to scratch his brain, too. First of all, would the vratches really be able to escape to the wilderness preserve? That depended on so many things that seemed unlikely now. Why had Richard been so sure that the vratches would be able to read a map? Richard knew kids in his class at school who couldn't read a map.

Then there were the puppy costumes. Were they such good disguises for the vratches, after all? They would fit, Richard was pretty sure of that. And if anyone caught sight of a vratch in a puppy suit, they wouldn't think it was a vratch. But what *would* they think—that a nursery school class was taking a field trip in the desert in the middle of the night?

Richard twisted onto his side and pulled the sheet over his head, but more gloomy thoughts seeped into his mind like poisonous gas. What had happened to Tony? After Tony's parents got through punishing him, they would want to make sure Richard was punished, too. Why hadn't they called Mom and Dad by now? He strained his ears, waiting to hear the telephone ring.

No, that was silly. It was after eleven—they would have called before now. Why hadn't they?

A startling idea struck Richard. They hadn't called because Tony, in spite of being so mad at Richard, hadn't told his parents that Richard helped steal the costumes. In fact, he might even have told them Richard had nothing to do with it.

That Tony Heckman. Richard had to give him credit. He was a pain, and he was completely unreasonable, but he was a good kid. Richard wished that Tony thought *he* was a good kid. He squirmed, as if he could rub off his guilt on the bedclothes. He should confess to his parents and the Heckmans the first thing in the morning, and take his medicine.

But if he did that, Mom and Dad certainly wouldn't allow him to go to the cryptozoology meeting. He would lose his only chance of finding Dr. Mounce and stopping Dr. MacNary.

Flopping onto his back again, Richard wished that this were last night and that Buck were sleeping in his room. Or what if it were tonight, but right now Richard would hear a throaty sound—*vratch, vraatch*—outside his window, and the screen wires strumming as Buck squeezed through. Buck would jump down into Richard's room, and they would dance around until Richard felt light and cheerful again.

Then he and Buck would draw pictures back and forth until they had worked out a brilliant plan for defeating Dr. MacNary and keeping the vratches safe forever. A plan so that Buck could keep on living in the canyon up in the hills, and Richard could hike up to visit him every now and then, bringing little presents like margarine cartons full of snails.

But of course Buck must be far across the desert by now, leading the other vratches to safety. Richard would have to do what he could all by himself. Without Tony, without Buck.

"Richard, why are you standing there with your mouth open, staring into space?" asked his father. He poured syrup on a waffle. "You'd better put your tie on. Don't keep Mrs. V. waiting—isn't that her, honking in the driveway? It's very nice of her to—"

Richard shook himself out of his sleepy fog. It had been an unpleasant shock when his radio woke him up this morning. "A tie?" he exclaimed. "I have to wear a tie, too?"

Richard felt foolish, walking out to Mrs. VanNest's car in his only sport coat, too short in the sleeves, and his stupid, striped clip-on tie. His mother had gotten them for Richard to wear to his cousin's wedding last spring. At least he had his Swiss Army knife in his slacks pocket.

Mrs. VanNest, dressed in a suit and flowered scarf,

beamed at him. She pulled her purse and tote bag over on the seat to make room. "Aren't you the dandy! I'll be so proud to walk into the conference with you and the keynote speaker."

"The keynote speaker?" asked Richard. Climbing into her gleaming purple car, he sank into the plush seat. "Who's that?"

"Dr. MacNary, of course." Mrs. VanNest began to back out of the driveway.

Richard stared at her, horrified.

"I knew you'd be excited, too. I offered to give him a ride to Riverside since his old station wagon isn't working very well. I'm going to interview him on the way." She tapped the tape recorder on the seat between them. "You won't mind hopping in the backseat when Dr. MacNary gets in, will you?"

At first Richard wondered whether he should hop out altogether and try to catch a bus to Riverside. But then he calmed himself. After all, Dr. MacNary didn't know Richard had found out about his surprise exhibit.

"This is Richard," said Mrs. VanNest as Dr. MacNary opened the car door in front of the Lagarto Palms. "The young man with the imagination that just won't quit. He's thrilled you're going to use his picture of the ornithoid in your presentation."

"So am I," said the cryptozoologist, placing a closed carton on the floor of the front seat. He stooped into the car, leaning an arm on the back of his seat, to take a careful look at Richard. Richard was sure he saw a gleam of recognition in the man's boiled-looking eyes.

Dr. MacNary turned and slid into his seat. "Isn't it ironic," he remarked as he fastened his seat belt, "that those who attempt to obstruct the progress of science often end up helping it?"

"I guess so," said Mrs. VanNest in a puzzled tone. "You must mean Dr. Mounce. Well! Ready for the interview? Before we get on the freeway, I'm going to turn on the tape recorder."

Mrs. VanNest's questions and Dr. MacNary's answers, mostly about how brilliant Dr. MacNary was, were not interesting to Richard. He gazed out the window at the hills sliding into the distance and the flat expanses of houses and apartments and factories beside the freeway. Which way was the Turtle Mountain Wilderness Preserve? Were Buck and the other vratches there now, searching the canyons for a new home?

Richard turned his head from the window and craned his neck to look at the carton, sealed with strapping tape, on the floor in front. That must be the surprise exhibit, the large bird skull with alligator teeth glued into it. Richard wondered if he should try to do something, like diving into the front seat and grabbing the carton.

That was what Richard would do if he were like the original Buck in *The Call of the Wild,* the "dominant primodial beast" going for the throat. Or if he were Tony, and not so afraid of getting in trouble. He'd slash the strapping tape with the large blade of his Swiss Army knife, grab the skull from the carton, and fling it out the window to smash to smithereens on the road. Then Dr. MacNary couldn't use it to prove to the other scientists that he was on the right track.

Richard pressed a button on the door to open his window.

"Let's keep the windows up, hon." Glancing at him in the rearview mirror, Mrs. VanNest pressed a button in the front seat to shut his window. "The wind makes too much noise to tape the interview." She turned back to Dr. MacNary. "You were explaining how other scientists—I can't actually name Dr. Mounce in the newspaper, of course—have held back your career because of jealousy . . ."

Richard leaned back against the plush cushions. It was just as well. Throwing the skull out the window wouldn't keep Dr. MacNary from making his speech or from leading his search party over the hills tomorrow. But it would almost certainly keep Richard from getting to the conference and talking to Dr. Mounce.

As they swung off the freeway, Richard noticed the message on the tall sign of the Ramada Inn: WELCOME CRYPTOZOOLOGICAL ASSOCIATION. "Here we are!" said Mrs. VanNest.

From the lobby of the Ramada Inn they followed the signs to the conference room, where a crowd was milling around long tables. "I have to register as a member of the press," said Mrs. VanNest importantly. "Here's a name tag for you, Richard." Dr. MacNary, carrying his carton, strode off toward the platform.

Peeling off the back of the sticky label (HELLO—my name is Richard Hayes), Richard was thankful that all these people had to wear their names on their chests. He had been afraid he would have to go around asking where Dr. Mounce was. On the other hand, there were a lot more people than he had imagined. And it wasn't so easy to get a clear view of their name tags.

Richard edged his way among the groups of talking

men and women. He developed a method of squeezing his way into clusters long enough to read all the name tags before he ducked out again. Some people frowned at him, but most of them didn't notice him at all. Now and then he caught sight of Mrs. VanNest, also squeezing her way into groups and poking the microphone of her tape recorder into someone's face.

The trouble was, Richard realized, he was missing a lot of people, because late arrivals kept coming up to the registration tables. How could he tell who he had checked? Starting to feel worried, he wormed his way back to the entrance. He would hang around and watch the name tags as they put them on. If only Tony were here, he could check the people arriving while Richard checked the people already in the hall.

"Richard, where have you been?" Mrs. VanNest seized his wrist. "Don't get lost on me! Come on, we have to sit down by the projector. Dr. MacNary will begin his speech in just a few minutes."

11

Going to the Offense

Richard felt like yanking himself away from Mrs. VanNest and running screaming through the hall: "Dr. Mounce! Dr. Mounce!" But instead he trotted alongside her to the back row on the center aisle. A bony-jawed woman in a limp gray suit moved down a chair so that Richard could sit beside Mrs. VanNest.

"Aren't you a little young to be attending a scientific conference?" the woman asked him.

Richard shrugged, embarrassed. He wondered if she might know Dr. Mounce.

The woman smiled sarcastically, the corners of her mouth pulling down. "Just don't believe everything you hear today. Especially from him." She nodded toward the stage, where Dr. MacNary was shaking hands with a bearded man. "He tried to prevent the *Cryptozoological Journal* from printing my findings on the supposedly extinct warbling pygmy ostrich—that's the kind of scientist *he* is."

Mrs. VanNest, who had been fiddling with the projector, gave the woman a cold glance. Taking a manila envelope marked *Ornithoid Project* out of her tote bag, she spoke to Richard. "Dr. MacNary said I was the only person at the conference that he would trust with his visual aids. I can see why—there's so much professional jealousy."

Richard braced his feet on the rung of his folding chair and pushed himself half up to watch the people trickling into the rows. He couldn't read any name tags from here. If only he had some idea of what Dr. Mounce looked like! He might be the young man across the aisle with the glasses held together at the earpiece with a safety pin. He might be the man with long white hair to the far left, gazing up at the ceiling and forming words silently. There was no way of telling.

At the front of the room, Richard noticed, Dr. MacNary's carton sat on one of the folding chairs behind the podium. Dr. MacNary was still talking to the bearded man. A young man in a denim jacket, a video camera on his shoulder, tried sighting at them from different angles.

"We may be on television, Richard!" Mrs. VanNest nodded toward the stage. "I *thought* the media might want to cover this. Look, they're setting up those bright lights. Dr. MacNary really ought to be wearing a little makeup to even out his skin tones."

Richard couldn't help thinking that it would take more than a little makeup to make Dr. MacNary look normal. But the sight of the TV crew worried him. It was bad enough that the cryptozoologist was going to talk all the scientists at this conference into heading for the hills to track down ornithoids. With TV coverage, he'd have half the people in Lagarto Grande County.

"I hope Dr. MacNary has these in order," remarked Mrs. VanNest, sliding a sheaf of drawings out of the envelope labeled *Ornithoid Project*. "Oh, yes, he has them all numbered." She stood up again. "Richard, you keep an eye on these things. I'm going to go up to the platform and see if I can set up my tape recorder there. It won't pick up the speech at this distance."

Feeling frantic, Richard took one last look around the room. Why had he been so sure that he could defeat Dr. MacNary if only he could come to the conference? It was hopeless. He might very well sit through the whole conference without ever finding Dr. Mounce. Then what?

Then Dr. MacNary would lead his hunt over Richard's hills, over the rocky places where Richard had found his quartz and mica, over the dip in the trail where Richard had met the deer. They would drive stakes with red tags into the ground beside the very bush where the vratch sentry had doodled a picture in the dirt.

They would clamber down into Canyon Vratch, to find—what would they find? All those people, including trained scientists who spent their time looking for rare animals, would certainly discover *some* trace of the vratches. Richard couldn't believe they wouldn't. And so after they'd ruined his hills, they'd follow the vratches to the wilderness.

An image came to Richard's mind, an image of Buck gazing at him with his large, dark eyes through the bars of a cage. Richard felt sick and cold. Buck would think Richard had let him down. There would be no way for Richard to explain how hard he had tried.

How hard he had tried? In the picture inside Richard's

head, Buck stared at him. His look seemed to say, You aren't trying. You're sitting there like a jerk.

His heart pounding, his jaw set, Richard half rose from his chair. He would march to the front of the room, jump onto the steps, and shout for Dr. Mounce.

With a groan Richard sank back into his seat. He couldn't leave the projector. Mrs. VanNest would be really mad if anything happened to her tote bag or to Dr. MacNary's pictures.

If anything happened to Dr. MacNary's pictures.

Richard clutched the edge of his folding chair, sparks going off in his mind until his whole head tingled. *That* was the way to do it. He, Richard, could make something happen to Dr. MacNary's pictures. He could send a picture message to Dr. Mounce. To all these scientists.

But . . . this was going to get Richard into much worse trouble than leaving his seat. Richard wished Tony were here. He could imagine him bouncing around like a boxer, head thrust forward, "Go to the offense!"

Putting his hand in his pocket, Richard touched the hard handle of his Swiss Army knife as if it were a good-luck charm. Then, his mouth dry, he glanced up at the podium. Mrs. VanNest was talking eagerly with the bearded man and Dr. MacNary—good. He dug into her tote bag, scrabbling to feel something long and thin. "A pen," he muttered.

"Need a pen?" The bony-faced woman next to Richard held open the coat of her limp gray suit, showing a plastic pocket protector bristling with pens. "Black felt-tip okay?" She handed it to him.

"Oh, thanks," gasped Richard. "Thanks very much."

As he opened the manila envelope of pictures, Richard thought the woman in the gray suit must wonder what in the world he was doing. He tried to put on a matter-of-fact, serious expression, as if of course he was supposed to be shuffling through Dr. MacNary's visual aids. There were sketches of Indian jars with the Great Lizard Spirit design, sketches of skulls and skeletons.

Richard drew in a deep breath. The last picture, number ten, was his. Dr. MacNary had lettered a caption underneath it: *Artist's Conception of the Ornithoid*. The vratch in the picture looked directly at Richard as if to say, I'm counting on you.

Pressing his lips together, Richard crossed out the artist's conception of an Ornithoid. He turned the paper over, wrote a number ten up in the right-hand corner as if this were the real visual aid number ten, and began to sketch. At first his hand quivered, but he imagined Buck looking over his shoulder, guiding him with gentle nips, and his black strokes became quick and sure.

Just as Richard slipped the picture back into the envelope, Mrs. VanNest came bustling down the aisle to the projector. "He's going to start! The president of the association is introducing him."

At the podium the man with the beard began to drone into the microphone: ". . . welcome you all . . . our distinguished speaker, Dr. MacNary . . ."

Dr. MacNary stepped to the mike, cleared his throat, and began to speak in a monotonous, professorlike tone. But a little smile played around his mouth as he enjoyed the thought of astounding the audience with his discovery. From time to time he nodded at Mrs. VanNest to change the picture in the opaque projector. Richard couldn't understand what Dr. MacNary was saying, since it was all in words like "documented by aboriginal artifacts" and "separate and highly specialized line of the class Reptilia."

It was warm and stuffy in the hall, and the glare of the TV lights made Richard's eyes tired. He hadn't slept much last night, between his middle-of-the-night guilt pangs and having to get up early. I can listen just as well with my eyes closed, he thought.

"He's a genius!"

Richard woke with a start. The man across the aisle with the safety-pinned glasses was leaning forward, fixing Dr. MacNary with an admiring stare. All around the room there were excited comments.

Dr. MacNary, smiling a satisfied smile, nodded toward the projector. Mrs. VanNest slid a drawing labeled *Skeleton of an Ornithoid* into the machine. Richard glanced anxiously from her to the screen and back again. That picture in the projector was number nine. What if she noticed something funny about number ten before she put it in the projector? What if she stopped and asked Dr. MacNary if the back was supposed to be crossed out? What if—

Mrs. VanNest beamed at Richard. "Isn't this thrilling?" she whispered. "A major scientific discovery in the making, and here we are right in the middle of it. It's almost like a—a spiritual experience." She looked up to see Dr. MacNary nodding at her for the next picture. "Oh! I'm not paying attention." Hurriedly she slipped the last picture out of the envelope and into the projector.

Dr. MacNary kept on talking, but a buzz began to grow in the conference hall. Now the woman on the other side of Richard was squinting at the screen, her mouth open. "Why, that's an ostrich skull. And a reptile skull—a young alligator? I should have known it! MacNary's transplanted the teeth!" Jumping up, she forced her way past Richard and Mrs. VanNest into the aisle.

Richard felt warm with pride. He had been afraid that he might not have drawn the scene well enough, but it seemed that the audience got the point. All around, people were exclaiming to their neighbors, pointing to the screen.

His boiled face puckered by a puzzled frown, Dr. MacNary turned toward the screen. Now he saw what everyone else in the conference hall was looking at, what Richard had seen last night, peering through the bamboo shade into Dr. MacNary's kitchen. There on the screen, larger than life, was Dr. MacNary in his shirt and tie and polka-dot boxer shorts. Hunched over the two skulls, he was transplanting teeth with a pair of pliers and a bottle of glue.

"This is a most annoying practical joke," began Dr. MacNary, his voice cracking. "Professional jealousy—"

But the woman in the gray suit was running up the steps to the platform, pouncing at the podium, tipping the microphone away from Dr. MacNary. "Twyla Mounce, ornithologist. I challenge Wade MacNary to let me examine this 'ornithoid' skull he says he discovered in the Lagarto Grande hills. Is this the box, Dr. MacNary?"

Over MacNary's protests, Dr. Mounce ripped off the strapping tape and unwrapped the skull. She peered at it from every angle, then waved her hand to quiet the buzzing audience. As the bright TV lights shone on her, and the TV cameraman pointed the camera at her, she held the skull up high.

Her crisp voice rang through the P.A. system. "Ladies and gentlemen, Dr. MacNary's great discovery: how to set alligator teeth into an ostrich beak with Elmer's glue."

Richard slumped back with a long sigh of relief. He thought, *We did it, Buck*.

12

Some Friend

Mrs. VanNest left the conference much earlier than she had expected to—without Dr. MacNary. "He can ride an ornithoid home," she snapped, pushing her way back from the platform with her tape recorder. "Are you ready to go, Richard?"

When they were on the freeway again, she began muttering, more to herself than to Richard. "Who would have thought he was such an unbalanced, even criminal, kind of person? Granted, he *was* wearing white socks with black shoes, but . . ." She glanced over at Richard. "I'm sorry, hon. I'm so upset that I forgot about you. You must be awfully disappointed to miss the talks about the Abominable Snowman and so on. Let's stop and have something yummy for lunch—I don't want you to feel you came all the way to Riverside for nothing."

"Oh, I don't feel that way," said Richard graciously. "But lunch would be nice—there's a Denny's."

On the way home, Richard's first thought was how much fun it would be to tell Tony about Dr. MacNary's downfall. But then he remembered how mad Tony was at Richard last night, and wondered uneasily what kind of punishment Tony's father had given him. Tony might be even madder now.

Still, when Mrs. VanNest dropped him off in his driveway, Richard ran straight over to the Heckmans' and knocked on the side door.

Mr. Heckman's heavy shoulders filled the doorway.

"Hi," said Richard. "Is Tony here?"

"Yeah. He is. In his room. He's going to stay there for a while, too. And he isn't going to see any friends."

"Oh." Richard wasn't really surprised. "Couldn't I just—"

He broke off as Mr. Heckman opened the screen door. But instead of letting Richard in, Tony's father shoved two wrinkled dark green trash bags at him. "Maybe *you* know what happened to the costumes that were in these."

Richard didn't know what to say. The plastic felt dusty in his hands, and bits of dry leaves fell out of the wrinkles.

"Tony tells me he sneaked them into the hills by himself, just for fun," Mr. Heckman went on. "Says he doesn't have any idea where they disappeared to." He stared steadily at Richard. "I made him take me up there this morning, and we looked all over the canyon where he said he left them—but all we found was these bags."

This morning would have been too early, probably, said Richard to himself. He couldn't have gotten them back by then.

"You take those bags home and think for a while

about how to fill them up.'' Mr. Heckman was pushing his jaw forward, just the way Tony did. ''Maybe you'll remember what happened to the costumes before I have to call your father.''

Smiling weakly, Richard backed away. He pretended to leave the Heckmans', then doubled around, behind the mock orange bushes bordering the driveway, into the back yard. He tapped on what he thought was Tony's window, although it was too high for him to see into the room. After a moment Tony's face appeared. Get out of here, he mouthed.

But Richard stood there, tapping, until Tony cranked the window open. ''Boy, you look so stupid with that tie on. And that name tag. 'Hello my name is Richard Hayes, jerkball.' ''

Richard flushed, pulling off the tie and name tag. ''Listen, I'm sorry about—''

''Where's the costumes?'' hissed Tony.

Richard was taken aback. ''You don't think—''

''Don't give me any baloney, Hayes. My dad and I looked under the bush and all over the canyon, and they weren't there. He's still deciding what he's going to do to me—staying in my room is just the beginning.''

''But—'' Richard stumbled over his words, eager to make Tony as happy and excited as he was. ''But you didn't allow enough time for Buck to bring the costumes back. They're probably up there now. I'll go look.'' He held up the trash bags. ''But listen—I made the biggest fool of Dr. MacNary! And I found Dr. Mounce, only it was a woman, not a man like we thought. And nobody's going to believe anything MacNary says ever again. So the vratches—''

"Isn't that just zippety-doo-dah," interrupted Tony. *"I'm* staying here until I tell where the costumes are—or until I rot."

Richard felt the excitement draining from him. "Not until you *rot*."

"That's what my dad said. He's madder than he was the time I put peanut butter in the carburetor. Some friend *you* are."

"But I asked Buck to bring them—"

His face tight with fury, Tony cranked the window shut.

Richard was left facing the blank stucco wall below Tony's window. He felt suddenly tired. He hadn't even gotten to tell Tony about Dr. MacNary up there on the screen in his underwear.

He walked back across the street, scuffing the loose grit on the pavement. Some friend *you* are, Tony had said. Funny, Richard hadn't exactly thought of Tony as a friend. He was just a kid Richard had started doing things with.

What if Buck *hadn't* returned the costumes?

That was a good question. Especially since, Richard realized now, returning them would be a lot of trouble for Buck.

He'd have to lug them all the way back from the wilderness preserve. Richard didn't know exactly how far away the Turtle Mountains were or how fast vratches could travel. He supposed that under cover of darkness, in the desert, they could stop pretending to walk like dogs and bound along on their hind legs. But how could Buck carry the costumes when he didn't even have the bags? Maybe he could replace the stuffing in his dog disguise with puppy suits. And he could get another vratch to come with him part of the way.

The trouble was, Buck couldn't possibly know how important the costumes were to Richard and Tony. How *could* he know how angry Mr. and Mrs. Heckman would be with Tony because Kimmy and the other little kids couldn't put on their costumes tomorrow and dance the Dance of the Puppy Dogs for their parents? How could Buck know that Tony thought Richard had betrayed him, just to play a game about an imaginary animal? Buck couldn't.

All Buck knew was that Richard had asked him to bring the costumes back.

Richard paused in the middle of his driveway for a moment, smoothing the wrinkled trash bags and gazing up at the steep folds of the hills. He felt like going in the house and flopping on the sofa. But there was no question about it—he had to look for the costumes. Hauling himself over the fence, he clambered up the cut into the sagebrush.

Richard was disobeying his parents again, hiking by himself. But that didn't matter very much now. This would probably be his last hike, anyway. His parents wouldn't change their minds about letting him go hiking by himself. His companion ''dog'' Buck was gone. And Tony hated him.

Richard couldn't really blame Tony. Richard, thinking only about helping the vratches and not at all about what might happen to Tony, had talked him into stealing the costumes. Now Tony was in bad trouble, and he didn't even have the comfort of knowing they had helped the vratches. He didn't even believe in vratches.

At least Richard's hills were safe, and he had them to himself one last time. He drew in deep breaths of sage-scented air, but it didn't lift him up. The hills seemed empty, now that he knew the vratches were gone.

Richard began to feel cheated. All the trouble he had gone to for the vratches, and he had never gotten to see one! There were the pictures he and Buck had drawn, but anybody could look at the picture in the *Grande View*. It wasn't fair. He couldn't even talk to anyone about vratches, except Tony. No. No, Tony wouldn't talk to him about anything now, let alone vratches.

Richard's legs hoisted him up the trail, step after step. The farther he hiked, the less likely it seemed that he would find the costumes. He hiked all the way past the firebreak, to the dip in the trail and the nearby reddish bush. Then he hesitated, squeezing the crinkly plastic bags. He supposed that under that bush would be the first place to look.

Vraatch.

Richard's heart stopped. His gaze flicked to a feathery gray-green clump of sagebrush, a few yards away.

There was an animal half hidden in the sagebrush. A gray-green feathered animal. Something like a kangaroo, something like a crested ostrich. It was so funny looking that Richard laughed. It was so beautiful that his eyes smarted.

"Buck," he breathed.

For a long moment the vratch stood perfectly still, propped on his thick tail, holding his little hands in front of his chest, as if to let Richard take a good look. Richard, holding his breath, wanted time to stop right there, like a freeze-frame at the end of a movie.

But time moved on. Buck ducked down into the bushes and began scrambling and struggling with something brown and floppy. Richard took a step forward to see what it was, but Buck uttered a grating sound, like a growl, and Richard stopped.

Then Buck the awkward brown dog shambled out of the sagebrush. There was nothing showing of Buck the vratch except for his dark liquid eyes—and the gray-green feathers of his chest and belly gleaming through the open zipper.

Richard felt that Buck wanted something from him. He trembled with eagerness. "What is it, Buck?"

Raatch. Buck touched the dog nose to his open chest.

"Oh!" Richard's fingers unclenched, and the trash bags dropped to the ground. Trembling more than ever, he took a step toward Buck, hesitated, and stepped forward again. He stooped to his heels in front of the vratch, found the zipper pull, and slowly, slowly zipped up the dog suit. Buck's short, stiff chest feathers brushed the knuckles of his right hand.

As Richard tucked the zipper pull deep into the dog fur, Buck seized his hand in his jaws. Gently he shook it back and forth. And then, turning so quickly that his tail slapped Richard's shoulder, he bounded over the rise and was gone.

Gone.

Richard scrambled to his feet and ran a few yards up the trail. Then he stopped, panting. He shouldn't follow Buck, even if he could. But he wanted to howl, like a dog left behind.

Swallowing hard, blinking his wet eyes as he turned

back, Richard focused on something brown and furry in the bushes. A pile of puppy suits.

Richard let out a shaky sigh. "Thanks, Buck." He had forgotten all about the costumes.

Richard was still tired, and it was a long hike back with two bags full of puppy-dog costumes over his shoulders. The late afternoon sun shone in his eyes, and the plastic bags kept catching on twigs as he brushed through the narrow path.

He should be happy, since Buck and the vratches were safe and he had the costumes back, but his leftover problems weighed Richard down. For one thing, his parents were still going to wonder what had happened to Buck. Dad had said last night that if Buck didn't turn up, they would call the animal shelter and all the vets. Richard wished he could tell his parents not to bother, that Buck was all right.

Well, at least Mom and Dad wouldn't be too upset for themselves that Buck was gone. They had no idea that he was anything more than a bargain-table dog. Of course they would feel sorry for Richard, thinking he was sad that Buck was gone. And he *was* sad, thought Richard, his throat tightening. He didn't have to pretend that.

But the worst thing was about Tony. Richard remembered the expression on Tony's face yesterday afternoon when he had said, "We've got to stop that slime." Because of what Richard had done, probably nobody would ever see that serious, open look on Tony's face again.

That certainly wasn't the look on Tony's face now, Richard thought, as Tony sat by himself in his room with nothing to do but wonder what horrible punishment his father would think up. Richard staggered faster and faster down the trail, once tripping and sprawling, skinning his elbows.

As he finally plodded down his driveway and across the street to the Heckmans', Richard wondered if he might be too late. Maybe Mr. Heckman had already decided what awful punishment he was going to give Tony, and was giving it to him right now. Richard forced himself to run up the driveway, the costume bags tugging his aching arms at each step.

Kimmy opened the door. The little girl's chin, covered with spaghetti sauce or catsup, dropped. As Richard stepped inside and lowered the bags to the floor, she jerked one open. "Daddy!" she screamed. "Richard stoled the puppy-dog costumes!" Mr. Heckman hurried out of the kitchen, wiping his mouth, while Kimmy danced around the bags, waving a costume. "You were right, Daddy! Richard stoled them with Tony." Her curls bounced.

"Actually, we just borrowed them for a while," muttered Richard to the floor. He knew he had to take his medicine, but it was awful to think that he could never explain to the Heckmans what a good reason he had for taking the puppy costumes.

Mrs. Heckman, right behind her husband, looked even more astonished than Kimmy. "I never would have believed it. And all this time I thought Richard would be a good influence on Tony."

"Huh," said Mr. Heckman. "The quiet ones are the worst."

Pulling a costume from a bag, Mrs. Heckman shook

132

it out. "Ack!" She coughed. "They're covered with dust. And—what kind of stitching is this on the tail?"

Richard could see, as she examined the seam between the tail and the body, that the tail had been sewed on with a coarse fiber.

"Oh, for heaven's sake," Mrs. Heckman clicked her tongue, pinching the flat tail. *"Why* did you boys have to pull the stuffing out of the tails?"

This was not a question that Richard felt he could answer, but luckily at that moment Tony dashed out of the hall. The hopeful look on his face changed to a wide grin as he caught sight of the costume bags. "Hey! Look at that. Well." He glanced at Richard, still grinning as if he couldn't help it, and back at the bags. "All *right!"*

"Tony," said Kimmy, shaking her curls at him, "you should have *told* Daddy Richard stoled the costumes with you."

"What do you mean, 'all right'?" Mr. Heckman asked Tony. "Who said you could leave your room?"

Tony grinned at his father, too. "You did. You said I could come out when the costumes turned up. And the costumes turned up, so . . ." He picked up one of the furry puppy suits. "Man, they're all dusty. What—" His eyes caught Richard's, and his grin faded into a wondering expression.

"Yes, aren't they dusty," said Mrs. Heckman in a sarcastic tone. "Funny how that happens when you drag them all over the hills. You boys have a little work to do. First, you can run a few loads of laundry, and then you can put new stuffing in the tails. I'll call Richard's folks to let them know what's going on."

Mr. Heckman nodded. "That's letting these wise guys off easy. If I were your father," he added to Richard, "I'd give you what-for so you'd never forget it. Of course that's your dad's business."

Richard gulped and tried to smile politely. It was just as well, he thought, that Mr. Heckman wasn't his father.

But Tony didn't seem worried anymore about what his father might do. Shouldering a bag of costumes, he jerked his head at Richard. "Come on, Rich. Washie, washie, washie."

That was that, realized Richard with relief. Of course his parents would ground him or think up some other kind of punishment, but he had pretty much taken his medicine. Picking up the other bag of costumes, he tramped toward the laundry room behind his friend Tony.